One in Every Crowd

One in Every Crowd

stories

IVAN E. COYOTE

 ARSENAL PULP PRESS | VANCOUVER

ARSENAL PULP PRESS
Suite 101, 211 East Georgia St.
Vancouver, BC
Canada V6A 1Z6
arsenalpulp.com

The publisher gratefully acknowledges the support of the Canada
Council for the Arts and the British Columbia Arts Council for
its publishing program, and the Government of Canada (through
the Canada Book Fund) and the Government of British Columbia
(through the Book Publishing Tax Credit Program) for its publishing
activities.

This is a work of fiction. Any resemblance of characters to persons
either living or deceased is purely coincidental.

Some of these stories appeared in previous books by Ivan E. Coyote:
Close to Spider Man, Loose End, Missed Her, One Man's Trash, and *The
Slow Fix.* Earlier versions also appeared in *Xtra!*

Front cover illustration by Elisha Lim
Author photograph by Vivienne McMaster

Printed and bound in Canada

Library and Archives Canada Cataloguing in Publication:

Coyote, Ivan E. (Ivan Elizabeth), 1969-
       One in every crowd / Ivan E. Coyote.

Short stories.
Also issued in electronic format.
ISBN 978-1-55152-459-7

       I. Title.

PS8555.O99O525 2012   jC813'.6   C2012-901141-X

FSC
www.fsc.org
MIX
Paper from
responsible sources
FSC® C103214

This book is dedicated to Francis, Frances, Felice, and Zena, for making me make myself into a better human, and a better writer, and for making my world a more honest and beautiful place to live in. You are my teachers, my friends, my family, and my future, and this makes me feel lucky and blessed.

CONTENTS

Four: Kids I Met

Five: Folks I Felt It Necessary to School in Some Way or Another, with Varying Degrees of Success

Six: Wisdom I Found, Learned, or Was Given

Introduction

Dear Kid I Was:

Hey there. It's me. I mean you. It is you/me, writing to me/ you, from the future. We are almost forty-three, and I sure do wish there was a way for me to get this message from future me to past you, but so far, humankind hasn't invented anything like that yet, not that I know of, anyway, so all I can do is write this letter and put it in the front of this book, and just maybe it might help out some other poor kid who feels all alone, just like you and I did, way back when. I am hoping this letter might let them know that they are not the only one. Dear Every Kid Who Picks Up This Book: You are not the only one.

We graduated in 1987, you and I, who can believe it, but that was twenty-five years ago. I would tell you right now that the last quarter of a century has flown by, but I know you, and back then you/I wouldn't have believed me. Why? Because I am writing to the me I was in 1985, and you/we are fifteen years old, and smack dab in the middle of grade ten and graduation feels like five lifetimes from now. School sucks today, in fact, life sucks, too, and you are miserable. It is February, and last fall that thing went down with that dude you were dating (here in the future, what he did that night to us would technically be called date rape, by the way), and the two of you broke up, but he was the popular guy, and you were kind of dorky plus also brand new to that school and he was two years older and about to graduate and in almost every club or team or whatever, and now him and his whole group of jocks and pretty boys and their girlfriends don't invite you to any parties, but you know what? You are better off without them. Better off without him, for sure. But you already knew that. You're no dummy, past me. And you only get better, little buddy. Trust me on this one.

So, while I have your ear, I want to tell you a couple of really important things. First, school is more important than you even thought it was. And I don't mean this in a boring I know it all and I am here to tell you kind of adult way, I am talking in the just between you and me as equals kind of a way. Educating yourself right now is your ticket to options, my friend. And I know you. You like options. So trust me when I tell you finishing school is important. Even more important than your mom thinks it is, and you know how she feels about a higher education. Well, she is right. I am here (or is it there) to tell you that every single thing you will ever manage to learn, every skill, every course, every bit of school or college or university you attend is going to help you on your way to becoming exactly who we always dreamed of being.

And you dreamed big. We dreamed of being a writer and a musician. You knew you wanted to be a writer since grade seven, remember, that assignment for what's-his-face's class, the teacher with the chalk marks all around his front pockets, and sometimes even the crotch of his brown cords (why did that man own only one good pair of pants for school?), anyway, remember what's-his-name's English class, and how he made everybody write a short story? Remember how good it felt? Well, one day you will get to do this for a living. A good living, now, after all those years of hard work. In fact, I am sitting in my office in a small home that my wife and I own, and I am writing a story right now, to you, from the future. The view from here is beautiful. But we have to get through high school first, so hang in there, little buddy, you are almost there. I am not going to tell you it gets better, even though it sure did, because really, how is that going to help you get through grade ten?

What you need right now is information. You need someone to tell you it is okay to be you. And hope. You need hope, and someone to say hey, I know exactly what you are going through. So hey, here I am, and I know exactly what you are going through. And you are, as our dear departed gran once told us when I was you and you were very little, exactly who God meant you to be. And I am here with you. I get it, I do.

I went through it too, remember? I am you. How could I not know what you are going through right now?

Where was I? Oh yeah. Important things I need you to know. Or wish I had known then. Stuff I wish someone would have told me when I was you.

You know how you always loved Dolly Parton? Even though she was really your mom's favourite first, and that is supposedly kind of uncool, right, to have the same favourite records as your mother, but who cares? It is Dolly. And one day you will go on to learn that it turns out she really is very cool, and even better, she is a survivor. Dolly Parton came from poverty, like, real poverty, and recorded her first songs when she was thirteen years old. She worked and worked and was smart, and used her brains and her voice *and* her body and her big breasts, and she built something for herself. And for her family, too. She always took care of her family. We have that in common, you and me and Dolly. Anyway, Dolly has a quote I love, and I want you to hear it now, and know it. It goes:

"Find out who you are and do it on purpose."

So, how, you might ask me, do I find out who I am? Good question, my young friend. One of life's big ones, in fact. Some of the greatest thinkers in the history of humankind have put their noggins in gear to try to answer this one for us all.

I don't really have the perfect answer, but I will tell you one thing I figured out. Or maybe I read it, or saw someone else doing it and copied them, but here it is:

One surefire way to figure out who you are is to never listen to anyone else tell you who or what you can be. Never let someone else decide for you what you are capable of being. Remember when that one music teacher told you that girls don't make good drummers? Well, turns out he was wrong. I am here to tell you that he was very wrong about that. In many other ways he turned out to be a great saxophone teacher, but he was profoundly wrong about the drumming thing. Right now, future you is in an all-butch choir, and you are singing and drumming and strumming your bursting heart right out, and it is a beautiful thing. I only wish that we hadn't listened to the guy who told us when we were thirteen that girls couldn't play drums, because then I would have started playing them thirty years ago.

Remember when everyone in school called boys who liked drama class or played the flute or who wanted to be cheerleaders fags? You know that guy Corey from home economics class, and Michael, and that blond kid, his name started with a D, I forget his name? Remember how that blond kid did that dance number for a talent show that one time in grade nine, and he could really dance, remember him, his name started with a D, and you don't know this yet because it hasn't happened, and you might wanna sit down because I know you, you are sensitive and this next little bit of news I am bringing you from the future is going to tear your tender heart right out, but I need you to know that he will go on to shoot himself in his father's basement with a rifle one winter a couple years after we graduate. And Corey, he will asphyxiate himself in Yellowknife in a car inside a garage in the dark of a long northern winter and see, I don't think either of these boys had to die, and that is why I am going to ask you a favour. Oh, Michael will make it, by the way. In fact, Michael will turn out to be a real nice guy who works with your sister and grows orchids in his spare time. But those other two guys, well, it didn't have to go down the way it did with them.

Past me, I know you have not accepted this about yourself yet, but I am here to tell you that you are queer, and not only is this fact about us nothing to be ashamed of, it will go on to be one of the things that teaches future you/me so much about the world, and about what is really important. Things like love and truth and honesty and compassion and respecting others who are different than you and friendship and community and chosen family.

So I am going to need you to do me a favour, like I said. I need you to go and find those kids they are picking on even worse than they are picking on you right now. I need you to be kind to them. Even when this means taking a risk with what is left of your own coolness at school. I am asking you to be brave and stick up for those kids they are calling a fag or a dyke, I want you to stand up for and beside those kids that get pushed around and left out and picked over and picked on and made to feel less than worthy somehow. Have their back, and in turn, they will have yours. And together, you will be better than the bullies. Braver. Taller. Truer. More righteous. Someone you can look back on one day and be really proud of.

Because trust me, no one ever gets to be forty-three and thinks about their life and what it all means, and wishes that they had stood aside more often and allowed more injustice to happen to more already struggling kids while they were back in high school. That is not going to happen. But what will happen is that you are going to grow up and look back one day and be sorry for your silences, and regret the times you stood by and let someone be cruel to someone

14

else, or even worse, joined in on it all yourself. And I know what you are thinking. You are thinking that I don't get it, that I have forgotten how hard high school really is in your here and now, because it is my way back when now. But I have not forgotten. I know for a fact that standing up and doing the right thing when more popular or prettier or richer kids are doing the wrong thing, or worse, is some of the hardest shit you will ever have to do in our entire life. But it is so worth it. You don't know this yet, but one day we will travel all over the world talking to scared and lonely and bullied and brave and smart and talented queer youth. One day you and I will literally save a kid's life, maybe more than one, even maybe, if we keep it up. But I need you to take that first step for me earlier than I was brave enough to do when I was your age. You feel me? In a way, you are kind of my second chance at doing it better, kid, and I am counting on you. I believe you can do this.

I can't do it all over, but I can pass on some of what I have learned to you. So, to sum it all up, here it is again: Make art. Write stories. Don't pay any attention to the haters. Most of them will grow up to be adult haters, too, and they will not leave anything behind but a bad taste in your mouth as their legacy. You are capable of great things, and beautiful things, but you need to be strong. Please, don't ever let anyone tell you that you can't sing, or dance, or do math or play the drums or hockey or be a full-time working writer. You can and will one day grow up to be a writer who plays the drums while dancing and singing and counting, all at the same time.

School sucks sometimes. This is the plain truth of it. Parts of school, just like parts of society, are meant to train you to conform, to make you afraid to be anything else but just like everybody else. But look around. Kindness and compassion will reward you with so much more than your fear or apathy will. Trust your heart, it is a lot smarter than you know. Find out what moves you, and be it. Be brave. Be fearless. Be fabulous. Make me proud of us. I know you can do it. I am living proof that you can be anything you dream and work and fight to be. I wish someone had given me these words when I was still you, but they did not. So I am giving them to you now. What you do with them is, of course, completely up to you.

With much love and affection,

Ivan
February 9, 2012

P.S. Do us both a big favour, would you? Don't ever start smoking. I hate to admit it twice in the same letter, but our mother was right about that one, too. It *is* a filthy habit. We quit four years ago today, and we have never looked back.

One: Kid I Was

No Bikini

I had a sex change once, when I was six years old.

The Lions pool where I grew up smelled like every other swimming pool everywhere. That's the thing about pools. Same smell. Doesn't matter where you are.

It was summer swimming lessons, it was a little red badge with white trim we were all after: beginners, age five to seven. My mom had bought me a bikini.

It was one of those little girl bikinis, a two-piece, I guess you would call it. The top part fit like a tight cut-off t-shirt, red with blue squares on it, the bottoms were longer than panties but shorter than shorts, blue with red squares. I had tried it on the night before when my mom got home from work and found that if I raised both my arms completely above my head too quickly, the top would slide up over my flat chest and people could see my ... you-know-whats.

You'll have to watch out for that, my mother had stated, her concern making lines in her forehead, *maybe I should have got the one-piece, but all they had was yellow and pink left. You don't like yellow either, do you?*

Pink was out of the question. We had already established this.

So the blue and red two-piece it was going to have to be. I was an accomplished tomboy by this time, so I was used to hating my clothes.

It was so easy, the first time, that it didn't even feel like a crime. I just didn't wear the top part. There were lots of little boys still getting changed with their mothers, and nobody noticed me slipping out of my brown cords and striped t-shirt, and padding, bare-chested, out to the poolside alone.

Our swimming instructor was broad-shouldered and walked with her toes pointing out. She was a human bull-horn, bellowing all instructions to us and punctuating each sentence with sharp blasts on a silver whistle which hung about her bulging neck on a leather bootlace.

"Alright, beginners, everyone line up at the shallow end, boys here, girls here, come on come on come on, boys on the left, girls on the right."

It was that simple, and it only got easier after that.

I wore my trunks under my pants and changed in the boys' room after that first day. The short form of the birth name my parents bestowed me with was androgynous enough to allow my charade to proceed through the entire six weeks of swimming lessons, six weeks of boyhood, six weeks of bliss.

It was easier not to be afraid of things, like diving boards and cannonballs and backstrokes, when nobody expected you to be afraid.

It was easier to jump into the deep end when you didn't have to worry about your top sliding up over your ears. I didn't have to be ashamed of my naked nipples, because I had not covered them up in the first place. The water running over my shoulders and back felt simple, and natural, and good.

Six weeks lasts a long time when you are six years old, so in the beginning I guess I thought the summer would never really end, that grade two was still an age away. I guess I thought that swimming lessons would continue far enough into the future that I didn't need to worry about report card day.

Or maybe I didn't think at all.

"*He* is not afraid of water over his head?" my mom read aloud in the car on the way home. My dad was driving, eyes straight ahead on the road. "He can tread water without a flotation device?" Her eyes were narrow, and hard, and kept trying to catch mine in the rearview mirror. "Your *son* has successfully completed *his* beginner's and intermediate badges and is ready for *his* level one?"

I stared at the toes of my sneakers and said nothing.

"Now excuse me, young lady, but would you like to explain to me just exactly what you have done here? How many people you have lied to? Have you been parading about all summer half-naked?"

How could I explain to her that it wasn't what I had done, but what I didn't do? That I hadn't lied, because no one had asked? And that I had never, not once, felt naked?

"I can't believe you. You can't be trusted with a two-piece."

I said nothing all the way home. There was nothing to say. She was right. I couldn't be trusted with a two-piece. Not then, and not now.

Walks Like

The fabric of this memory is faded, its edges frayed by time.

The young girl who lived it is now just a ghost inside of me. I can remember only her bones; the skin and flesh of her are brought to me in the stories of others. Mothers, uncles, and aunts remind me of the kind of child I was then.

There was the smell of Christmas everywhere, I do remember that, pine trees and wood smoke and rum cake. The women smelled of gift perfume, the men of new sweaters.

Everywhere were voices, maybe a dozen different conversations woven together in the rise and fall of talk and laughter that is the backdrop of all my mind's snapshots of my family then, a huge room full of people connected to me by their blood.

I was sitting almost too close to the fire. Iced window panes separated us from the bitter white of winter outside. Everyone I'd ever known was still alive.

I was about four years old.

Both of my grandmothers sat in overstuffed chairs next to the fireplace, talking, a trace of Cockney, and a hint of an Irish lilt, respectively.

I sat on the thick rug between them, rolling a red metal fire truck up and down my white-stockinged legs, making motor, gear-changing, braking noises. Listening.

"You should have seen the fuss this morning, getting her into that dress. I tell you, Pat, I'd've never stood for it from any of my girls. You'd've thought I was boiling her in oil, the way she was carrying on. She wanted to wear those filthy brown corduroy pants again, imagine that, and she knows we're going to mass tonight." My mother's mother clicked her tongue and sent a stern glance in my general direction.

"That was what all my boys were like, Flo. Really, if you could have seen me the day that portrait on the wall there was taken, I swear I didn't have a nerve left for them to get on. Like pulling teeth, you know it was, to dress those four."

"Well, you'd expect it from the boys, you know, it's only natural. But her, I don't understand it. Her mother always liked to dress up, and never a speck of dirt could you find on my Norah ... look here, come here you." She curled an arthritic finger at me.

I stood up reluctantly and dragged my feet across the carpet toward her, hoping for a good spark.

"Look, see what I mean? Look at her knees, how does she do it? It's only been a couple of hours, and there's only snow on the ground out there. I couldn't find any dirt right now if I went out looking. Here, let me fix up that zipper ..."

My small fingers shot up to intercept her, and a rather large bolt of static electricity flashed between us. She pulled her gnarled hand back for a moment, and then brought it down on the back of mine. "What a nasty thing to do to your poor old gran! Aren't you ashamed of yourself? Now, run and fetch us both a rum ball, and for the love of Mary, don't get it all over the front of you."

I looked over to my other grandmother, at the shadow of an evil smile which pulled at the corners of her mouth. She winked at me, and motioned for me to be off.

"See what I mean about her, Pat? I'm worried sick she'll turn out to be an old maid. What happens when she starts school? Look, now … she even walks like a little boy …"

"You're far too hard on her, Flo," came the voice of the mother of my father from behind me, laced with just a hint of annoyance. "She will be just fine. She just walks like that. That's just how she walks."

Just Reward

She was never that good at Frisbee, but it wasn't about that for me. Her summer brown legs bent with a grace I could never possess, and her straight black hair swung unbraided, always a strand or two across her face, in her mouth.

Her palms were lighter than the backs of her hands, and often she would lay them in the place her hips would be one day, plant both feet in the dust, and throw her head back when she laughed.

She was doing just this the day we found the money. Her Frisbee throws were unpredictable and wobbly, and this one had arced sideways into the juniper bushes that lined the parking lot next to the parched park we were playing in.

Nothing is as dry as July dust in the land of the midnight sun, so I almost missed the brown leather wallet laying in the dirt.

"Valerie, come look here. Look at this."

"I don't want to look at bugs. Come on, throw it here."

She saw the look on my face and went silent, looked down into my hands.

A rectangle of worn calfskin with a brass bill clip inside, pinning down a wad of American bills. I stuffed it into the waistband of my shorts and we ran down to the edge of the river, under the cover of willows.

Eleven one hundred dollar bills, two twenties, four ones.

"One thousand, one hundred and forty-four dollars." Valerie was perched on the balls of her feet, her teeth shining white behind chapped lips. "We have to take it to the police station," she whispered.

"The police? Are you crazy? We could buy practically anything with this."

She shook her head, a wrinkle creasing her forehead. "Our parents would take it away anyhow. The police." She said this like there was no other option.

"We could hide it for a while then, in the fort. We could save for our educations." I appealed to her practical side.

"If we take it to the police, and they can't find whose money it is, then we can keep it. We could be heroes." She raised her eyebrows and rubbed her palms on her shorts for emphasis. "Rich heroes."

It was settled then. I never once thought to argue that it was I who had found the money. I had no name for what I felt for her; we were nine years old and I would have done anything she wanted.

"You fucking did what?" My father was chewing his pork chop with his mouth open.

My mom slapped his arm, right above where his shirtsleeve was rolled up to. "You did the right thing. I'm really proud of you girls, and so is Valerie's mom."

My father looked at me like he couldn't figure out just where he had gone wrong.

The policeman shook his head as he filled out the form. "Well, he was probably an American." This guy was sure to make detective. "No ID, huh?" He narrowed his eyes at us, beads of sweat on his forehead.

We shook our heads simultaneously.

"Beginning of summer, probably on his way up north. To Alaska," he explained, as though there was a multitude of destinations for tourists to choose from. "There's a chance he'll check in on his way back down. No one claims this in six weeks, say, then you two are in the money."

We spent that money over and over in our heads for the rest of the summer. Valerie wanted a camera, and an easel and paint set. "No cheap stuff. The kind of brushes with horse hair in them."

I wanted a BMX with chrome pedals, and a microscope. "Maybe a chemistry set, too. And walkie talkies. One for me, one for you. We could talk on them late at night. And a rowboat."

"Cowboy boots," she added, swinging in the hammock, a piece of straw between her front teeth. "Red cowboy boots."

It was the ninth of August. We had seven days left.

The next morning, the phone rang at exactly eight o'clock. I was eating puffed wheat and listening to "Seasons in the Sun" on the radio that sat between the toaster and the plant on the lemon yellow counter next to the window. My mom was filling the kettle, and held the phone between ear and shoulder, motioning silently at me to turn the music down. "She's right here. I see. Okay, I'll tell her. Thank you, officer." She uncurled the phone cord with her forefinger and hung it up. "Someone claimed the wallet. He's downtown, he wants to give you two a reward. I'll drop you both off on my way to work."

We sat side by each in the back seat of my mom's Tercel, silent and lead-bellied under our seat belts. Valerie smelled like Irish Spring soap and toothpaste. I had forgotten to even brush my hair.

He looked like a caricature of a tourist come magically to life. The buttons of his polyester print shirt strained to hold his belly inside his khaki shorts. He even had waxy hairs sticking out of his ears. He shook our hands, his moist palms unnaturally soft. "Here are my little heroes," he wheezed. He patted us both on our heads, mussing our hair and smiling at the cop behind the counter. "Let's head across the street and get you girls your re-ward."

He stood perspiring in the service window of the Dairy Queen. "What's your favourite flavour of milkshake?"

"She likes strawberry, chocolate for me," I piped up. Talking to strangers was my job. Explaining why we had done what we did to parents was her territory, but strangers were my area of expertise.

"Too early for milkshakes," she whispered to me, as he pulled out his billfold and handed over the four singles. I shushed her. Surely this was just the first phase of our reward.

But ten minutes later we sat alone at the bus stop, the

change from our milkshakes stuck to my palm, for bus fare. He had told us what good girls we were and hopped into his motor home. His wife had waved over her knitting at us from the passenger seat. The TravelEase edged back onto the road. "I hate South Carolina. Never going there." Valerie spit in the dust and tied up her shoe.

My dad was still at home when we got back, strange at this time of day. He was smoking an Export 'A', drinking tea, and reading *Shogun*. We tried to head straight into my room, but he looked up and cleared his throat.

"Whoawhoawhoa. Where're you two going?"

Valerie picked idly at a scratch on her thigh; I stood on one leg, then the other, waiting for the inevitable.

"Didja get your re-ward?" He split the word in two, like someone from South Carolina would.

I nodded almost without moving my head. Valerie shrugged.

"Welllll...?" His one eyebrow raised, his hands perched like spiders on the wooden table.

"We got milkshakes," Valerie said softly.

My dad turned his right ear to us, played with a make believe hearing aid.

"He bought us both milkshakes," I blurted out, the sweetness of chocolate already halfway back up my throat.

"Small or large?" he crowed, slamming both palms flat, slopping tea onto his paperback.

"Large ones." The bottom of Valerie's jaw stuck further out defiantly, her brown palms returning to her hips.

My dad laughed from deep in his belly at us both, and reached for his smokes. "Well I hope it went down good, because that was the most expensive fuckin' milkshake you're ever gonna drink."

Twenty years later I realized we had, in fact, spent that money on our educations.

It Doesn't Hurt

My cousin claims he invented the game, but I swear it was me. You need what they call a rat-tail comb, one of those plastic ones you can buy at the drug store; they come in bags of ten. They have a comb part, and then a skinny plastic handle, which, I suppose, is where the name comes from.

You take the comb and heat it up over an element on the stove so you can bend a curve into it, like a hockey stick. Then you get a ping pong ball, or one of those plastic golf balls with the holes, and there you are. Comb ball, we called it. Let the game begin.

The game was invented to be played in a long, narrow hallway, so a mobile home is the perfect stadium. You close all the bathroom and bedroom doors, and each opponent gets on their knees at either end of the hall. Kind of like a soccer goalie, only shorter. Whoever has the ball goes first.

You hold the handle of the comb in one hand and bend the comb back with the other, and let go. The ping pong ball rebounds off the walls and floor at speeds approaching the sound barrier, and the other guy tries to block the ball with any part of his completely unprotected body.

A ping pong ball striking naked skin at the speed of sound is bound to hurt. So there were the obvious injuries: circular welts about the face, neck, and arms were common.

There were other hazards, too: carpet burn, bruised elbows and knees. Once, my sister leapt up to block a shot and smashed her head on a door handle and just about bit the tip of her tongue off. My cousin sprained his wrist trying to flip himself back onto his feet for a rebound.

My aunt stepped in, in an attempt to reduce the casualties. She tried to ban comb ball altogether, but was met with such a united front of dismay and pouting that she was forced to compromise. We were only allowed to play until someone cried. And we had to scrub off all the little white marks the ping pong balls left on the wood panelling.

We were only allowed to play until someone cried. Of course, this added a masochistic element to the game we all enjoyed. I would take a stinging shot to the lower lip and kneel motionless in the hallway, breathing deep through clenched teeth. Everyone would stop, searching my face for any sign of moisture, which would signal the end of the game. "Doesn't hurt," I would whisper bravely. "It doesn't hurt. It doesn't hurt. Let's go. My shot." Everyone would let out their breath and continue.

Whoever cried ended the game. Whoever cried sucked. My aunt would march in and grab our combs, and send us outside to play. "It's a beautiful day out there. Quit killing each other in my hallway and go get some exercise."

Playing outside was okay, but there was nothing like a rousing, bloody match of comb ball. We would compare scars afterwards, like soldiers. "Took the skin right off, bled all over the rug too," we would brag, our striped shirts pulled up over our elbows. "And not one tear. Kept right on going."

My cousin Christopher ended it all the day he broke his thumb. This required a trip to emergency, and a splint. He forgot to try not to cry, and the combs were confiscated for good. For a while we were impressed with his sling, and his need for painkillers, but then reality set in. No more comb ball. Christopher was a wimp, and prone to accidents. Remember, he got that concussion that one time and they took the tire swing away? We all mourned the loss of the greatest game that ever came to the trailer park.

We came up with a version of cops and robbers that satisfied our bloodlust for a while. It involved riding around on our bikes and wailing on each other with broken-off car antennas, but it wasn't the same. Crying while playing outside was a different story, because you got to go back into the house. The stakes weren't as high. There was nothing to lose.

I worry today, about my friends' kids. Nothing hurts when you play Nintendo, not even when you die. What are we teaching our children? I still utilize the skills I learned playing comb ball. Just the other day, I fell off the back of a five-ton truck helping my friend move. I leapt up immediately, exclaiming, "It doesn't hurt. It doesn't hurt." And a couple of weeks later, it didn't. Just like the good old days.

Sticks and Stones

It seemed like a fine idea at the time. Of course, now I look back and count my ten fingers and toes, my two legs and arms that still function properly, shake my head that sits on top of the neck I have never broken, and thank my guardian angel that I still possess these blessings. But it seemed like a fine idea at the time.

My father is a welder, and his shop was located in the middle of a large and potholed industrial section just off the Alaska Highway on the edge of town. It came complete with snarling guard dogs and broken-down bulldozers, and even had its very own forgotten car and truck graveyard. If you looked up from the dusty ground and buckets of used oil, out behind colourless mechanics' shops and the skeletons of scaffolding, you could see the whole valley stretched out, the Yukon River sparkling blue and snaking through the painted postcard mountains. If you looked up, which I rarely did. There was too much to do.

There were any number of stupid and dangerous activities to pass the day with, untold numbers of rusty edges to tear your skin and clothes on, a myriad of heavy metal objects to fall off of or get pinned beneath. I don't remember whose idea the tires were. They were not just any tires;

they had once pounded dust under earth movers, or dump trucks. They were monsters, and they were everywhere. It took the whole pack of mechanics' kids and welders' daughters and crane operators' sons to move them; getting them up and onto their sides was a feat of team effort and determination, aided by crowbars we pinched from the backs of our dads' pick-ups when no one was looking. Rolling them to the edge of the power line without being noticed involved lookouts and quick action. We knew they would stop us if they found out; we didn't need to ask. The covert element of the operation only added to the thrill of it all.

Only two of us could fit in at a time, which was okay, because we had all summer and plenty of tires. Three or four kids would hold the tire steady, teetering on the edge of the cliff at the top of the power line, and two would climb inside. Kind of like gerbils on one of those exercise wheels, except you would face each other, arms and legs pushing out into the inside of the tire to hold yourself in. Gravity pretty much took care of the rest.

It was better than any roller coaster, not that any of us had been on one. It was the random element of the tire's path that did it. There was just no way to know what that tire was going to bump into or off of, and the only thing more fun than the roll down was when the tire started to come to a stop at the bottom, and did that roll-on-its-side, flip-flop dance at the bottom of the hill, kind of like a coin does when you flip it and miss and it lands on the linoleum. Only this was a huge dump truck tire with two dirty kids inside, laughing hysterically, laughing until tears ran and our sides hurt the next day. Only one of us ever puked: the heavy duty mechanic's oldest daughter lost her lunch all over her brother one day, and so we never let her ride after that, just sent her into her dad's shop to distract him while we rolled tires past his big bay doors out front.

I think it was the smell that finally gave us away. My mom kept asking me what the hell had I been up to that day while my dad was at work. There is something unmistakably foul about the smell of the inside of a tire, a cross between pond water and cat pee, I would venture, and my mom couldn't quite pin it down, but she got suspicious.

It was a bright August morning, the day it all ended, and we had a beauty of a big tire all loaded up and ready for take-off when we heard a noise inside our heads, a skull-piercing shriek that stopped our blood. We all froze in our tracks. My mom appeared from out of nowhere and it dawned on me that the noise was originating from her mouth, the words becoming slowly recognizable as she bee-lined toward us, her face all veins bulging red, and the whites of her eyes all you could see: "*What the fuck are you stop right now stop that stop it stop ...*" and so forth.

There was really no explaining our way out of this one. What else could we possibly have had in mind? More damning, of course, was the pile of tires already situated at the bottom of the power line; we couldn't even argue that we were just thinking about climbing inside one and rolling it down the hill, but were just about to prudently change our minds and go help our fathers sort bolts and sweep up.

An ad-hoc committee of irate parents was called immediately, and our dads did what any fathers would have done when catching their child about to engage in activities which could only result in grievous bodily harm: they spanked us all senseless. Nothing like pain to remind you of how much you could have been hurt. It was, after all, the seventies. I was also given plenty of time to mull over my decisions for the next two weeks: I was grounded, and spent the rest of the summer inside at home, watching the Seventh Day Adventist kids safely ride their bikes on the road. What could you do? Like I said, it seemed like a fine idea at the time.

Bad Luck and Big Feet

We couldn't believe our luck that day we walked into the Sally Ann and saw all those roller skates. Story was, they had just shut down an old rink, and about two hundred pairs of kids' rental roller skates had been donated to the thrift store. The cool kind, too, where the translucent yellow wheels were bolted right to the soles of sturdy-looking running shoes that tied up with wide white shoelaces, not the dorky old-fashioned kind that you had to strap on over your own shoes and tighten up with a key that always went missing after a couple of days.

They were all on sale for a buck fifty a pair, because there were so many of them they were clogging up the entire sporting goods aisle, overflowing from the shelves and piled on top of a moth-bitten street hockey net.

Gran announced that she was going to buy all of us our very own roller skates, since they were a bargain, plus we had behaved ourselves all day so far. She told us we could go ahead and help ourselves to a pair that fit, but not to bother the poor lady behind the counter with it, she had enough on her plate as it was.

We all raced forward, digging about for the best-looking pair in our size, almost climbing over one another, like you see nowadays when they have half-price stuff on sale at the Wal-Mart or somewheres. The only thing better than getting new stuff was not having to share it with anyone. A few springs back Christopher got a skateboard for his birthday, and we all had to take turns on it. Chris wasn't exactly famous for sharing, and he knuckle-punched his brother for hogging it too long. My little sister ran into the house to tell on Chris and woke up my Uncle Kevin who ended up locking the skateboard in the trunk of his car, just so he could get some peace and quiet since he was working the night shift.

Four kids, and a hundred pairs of roller skates to pick from. Mine were blue, with three white racing stripes down each side. They were practically brand new, the wheels were just a tiny bit scuffed. The laces even had the little plastic tips on them still, like shiny back-to-school gym shoes do for the first half of September. Carrie wanted the yellow ones, but they were too big so she settled on red, and Danny's were a faded blue, at one time the same colour as mine, but now a little grey after being handled by a thousand different dirty fingers.

Now all we had to do was find a pair that fit Christopher. The thing about my cousin Christopher was that he was extremely prone to misfortune. My gran once even crossed herself and said that Chris must have slept in the morning that the good Lord was handing out the luck, because nobody else had ever choked on the only quarter hidden in his own birthday money cake. It was like he was born with a little dark ball of wrong turns and close calls and mishaps that hovered in a tangled cloud above his head, I swear, you could almost see its shadow on the sidewalk beside him some days. When bad luck decided that something needed to happen to someone, it usually picked Chris, since he was never more than an arm's length away from a catastrophe. Spilled milk, bee stings, and deep slivers followed him around like stray dogs. He couldn't help it; it wasn't his fault, he was just born like that.

When he first started kindergarten his teacher thought he might be slow, and they almost put Chris in the special class, until my aunt had to go down to the school and give that teacher a piece of her mind. Just because a kid didn't talk much didn't mean he couldn't count backwards from one hundred and already know his alphabet by heart. Not to mention how many slow kids could take a radio apart and put it back together when they were barely five years old and if that teacher had his head screwed on right he would know it. It turned out that Christopher was not part retarded (that's what they called it back then), he was just mostly deaf, but by the time the doctor put the tubes in his ears, the bullies and bigger kids had picked up the scent of blood in the water and closed in on my cousin. He was quiet, and clumsy, and something about the way he blinked his eyes and chewed his bottom lip showed his fear and evoked cruelty in others. He was all awkward elbows and not quite right angles, and his feet and hands looked like they belonged on a much bigger body, like he had recently borrowed them from a boy twice his size.

One hundred pairs of discount roller skates, yet somehow none that Christopher could squeeze his feet all the way into. His bottom lip swelled into a quivering pout, and his eyes filled up with tears.

I knew it was a sin to hate your own cousin just because he was born with bad luck and big feet, but I couldn't help it, and a sour ball of guilty spit got caught in my throat and refused to be swallowed.

"No fair if everyone gets roller skates but me." His voice sounded small, and broken. He picked at a scratch above his knee and rubbed one sock foot with the other. The rest of us stared down at the worn-out floor tiles and pondered this awful truth.

Gran's form of justice was swift, and thrifty. After enduring a brief bout of tears from all four of us, followed by a sobering sermon that included such topics as the mouths of gift horses, shoeless children from other countries, counting your blessings, and living on a fixed income, we were given two options. We could go home without any roller skates at all, or Gran would buy Carrie, Dan, and me each a used pair, and then we would take the bus to the mall and find a brand new pair that fit Christopher. Of course, we chose option #2.

At the sporting goods store, the only ones we could find were the old fashioned kind that you strapped on over your shoes and tightened with a key. Gran told the salesman that it was highway robbery, what he was charging her for them, and he gave her ten percent off, even though there was usually no senior's discount on sports equipment. It was obvious that she had almost had enough of the whole business, so Chris didn't dare complain that his skates weren't as cool as ours were, and we didn't risk even a sideways gloat.

The biggest patch of pavement in our neighbourhood was the parking lot beside the baseball diamond, about two blocks up the hill from our house. We wobbled and rolled up the road as soon as we got home, laughing and leaning on each other for balance. We stopped at the top of the hill for a minute to catch our breath. The street sloped down in a lazy curve and met the steeper road that led into the parking lot. Carrie went first, her bum sticking out and her feet spread too far apart, a squeal of glee trailing behind her as she picked up speed. Dan bent his knees and cannon-balled down the hill, almost overshooting the turn-off, and I followed just far enough behind to avoid rear-ending him. My eyes were fixed on the road, on the lookout for patches of dandelions that had pushed their way up through cracks in the chip-seal, and bits of gravel big enough to catch a wheel on.

It dawned on me that none of us had spent much time practicing how we were going to stop before starting down the hill, and as the oldest, this was just the kind of detail I should have thought about. Carrie hit the scruffy lawn and fell forward, her arms and legs splayed in all directions like a starfish. She curled into a ball, clutching the crotch of her shorts since she was prone to peeing herself when she got too excited. Dan managed to grab a signpost with one hand and spun to a stop, and I safely bounced off the tired chainlink fence that sagged around the outside of the ball diamond. Christopher hesitated at the top of the hill. The afternoon sun burned like an egg yolk in the blue behind him, and the air rippled in blurry waves wherever the sky touched the pavement. The toes of his sneakers stuck way out over the front wheels of his skates, and his naked knees were glued together. It crossed my mind that maybe letting the younger kids learn how to roller skate in bare legs was not such a good idea, but it was too late. Chris careened towards us, his arms whirling in giant circles, backpedaling on his heels in a slow-motion slapstick of panic. He fell on his butt and skidded to a stop not even halfway down the hill. There was a breathless second of silence, and then his jaw dropped and an animal sound came out of his open mouth. I had never heard anyone screech like that, it was worse than when Danny burnt his leg on the exhaust pipe of his dad's motorbike, even louder than the time I fell out of the tree and broke my wrist and got eleven stitches in my head. It was more of a siren than a scream, and he didn't stop. My blood stood still in my veins for a moment, then I leapt forward, forgetting I had wheels attached to my feet. I broke my fall with the heels of both hands, tearing identical patches of roadrash into my palms. I ripped both of his roller skates off, and ran my stinging hands up and down his arms and legs, searching his body for blood or broken bones. I pulled him to his feet by one elbow and a belt loop, but he sunk back into a crouch when I let go of his arm, still wailing and spewing tears and snot.

I couldn't see anything wrong with him, he wasn't bleeding or holding his ankle or wrist, but he was screaming like he was being skinned alive. When I knelt down beside him to wrap his arm around my shoulders, a foul smell filled my nostrils. He had crapped his pants, and the evidence had escaped his underwear and was smeared down the back of his right leg. I had to take him home, which meant I had to take everyone home, since it was 1981 and it wasn't safe to leave little kids alone in a park in a big city, especially when there was a psycho on the loose and anything could happen.

My sister wouldn't touch Christopher because he had poo on him, so I made her carry the roller skates while Dan and I dragged him home in our sock feet. He was made of lead and rubber, and by the time we burst through the screen door on the back porch my knees were wobbling and my breath was burning in the back of my throat.

"Gran," I gasped, "Chris wiped out on the hill and I can't see anything wrong with him but he pooped himself and won't shut up or tell me where it is hurting."

Chris had stopped screeching, but his chest still heaved in great long sobs and his face was streaked with dirt and tears. He wiped his upper lip with a snotty wrist, and leaned against the laundry room door, which wasn't closed all the way. It swung open with a squeak and Chris stumbled sideways and fell to one knee on the linoleum in front of the washing machine, leaving a brown streak of poop across the white ceramic door of Gran's brand new clothes dryer.

"You dirty little bird," she squawked, hauling Chris back onto his feet by one wrist and dragging him toward the bathroom. "Knock it off with all this nonsense and get into the tub or I'll give you something to cry about."

She launched him through the bathroom door with one

swat across the sagging bum of his shorts.

He let out a scream so loud that even Gran clapped her hands over her ears, and the dog bolted down the hall, skidded across the kitchen, and hurled herself under the table, knocking the butter dish to the floor. Not even my little sister could fake that kind of agony, and Gran lifted his limp body into the bathtub and pulled down his pants with a shaky hand. His bum was snow white, and between his poo-smeared butt cheeks bulged a giant purple egg. It was a horrible hybrid of a blood-blister and a bruise, and it throbbed and pulsed like a swollen creature from a science fiction movie. Even the nurse at the walk-in clinic in the mall claimed she had never seen anything quite like it, and said that she bet it hurt something terrible. Then she patted the sweaty curls on top of Chris's head with a manicured hand, and gave him an envelope that had twelve real painkillers in it, not just orange-flavoured baby aspirin, and a frozen bag full of what looked like blue jello.

Gran called us a cab from the pay phone outside of the 7-Eleven, even though the mall was only ten blocks or so from our house and we had no luggage or groceries. We were all acting super nice to Chris, since we felt bad for thinking he was being a big baby because it we had mistakenly thought he had barely wiped out at all because we couldn't see any blood or wounds, but how were we supposed to know he had a giant purple lump in his shorts that hurt so much it made him shit himself? My sister even gave him her winning Oh Henry! wrapper she had kept folded up in her pink plastic wallet for weeks. She had been waiting for the right time to trade it in for the free Pepsi she had coming, saving it for a rainy day, she said, which really meant a day when the rest of us were broke. Carrie was like that, she used to hoard a good chunk of her Halloween stash every year too, just so she could haul it out a month later and eat it with dramatic relish in front of the other kids without sharing. But she gave her free pop to Chris, and Gran let him sit in the front seat of the cab alone, and she made him a jam sandwich right before dinner, just because. Chris was good about it all, he didn't lord his injury over us able-bodied kids like some would, he didn't make us get him stuff or hog the couch or fake a limp so he wouldn't have to help with the dishes or go move the sprinkler. Gran watched him wince as he slowly settled himself onto a chair at dinnertime. He sat lopsided, perched painfully atop the blue ice pack, and laced his fingers together so we could say grace.

Gran thanked God for the meal we were about to eat, and made the sign of the cross. Then she picked up her fork and shook it at the four of us, clucking her tongue like she did when she was about to say how something was a crying shame.

"Look at him, poor little wretch. It's a crying shame none of yous had enough sense to put on long pants before you went out fooling around on them things, just a crying shame. Count yourself lucky that nobody cracked their skull wide open, thank Gawd." She looked up at the ceiling tiles, and crossed herself again.

We sat with our hands in our laps and our heads bowed,

just in case this particular crying shame needed any further explanation or perhaps an extra prayer. I mulled it all over in my head, wondering how long pants could possibly prevent head injuries, and whether or not Chris would still have got poop all over the dryer door if he had crapped in his jeans instead, and would any of this have happened at all if he hadn't been born with giant feet that only fit into the crappy roller skates? And didn't that mean the whole thing was in fact an act of God? I pressed my lips together to keep myself quiet. It was best not to ask too many questions, especially ones about the Good Lord Above. I was old enough to know it was a sin to blame God when bad things happened, even things that could only be his fault, like floods or earthquakes or innocent children from good homes who died too young or babies who got born with a rare disease or a weak heart. It was blasphemy to question his will or his wisdom or the way he went about his business, to even suggest that God might have thought twice before burdening a boy with feet that did nothing for his self-esteem which was a big part of why he had to repeat grade two and go see the special ed teacher for extra help with his math and spelling instead of going to gym class with all the other kids and that is why he sucked at almost every sport except wrestling and sprinting and long-distance running which he had plenty of practice at from getting chased home or beaten up.

The next day Gran took all four pairs of roller skates back to the Salvation Army and traded them in for a bat, three baseball gloves, and a grass-stained softball, even though Chris sucked at baseball too. The only fair thing to do was to give all of us something none of us wanted, and disappointing all of us equally was the only way to keep everyone happy. I knew it wasn't her fault that we had gotten on her last nerve and she had to wash her hands of it all and teach us a valuable lesson so we would think twice next time before risking our necks when she had enough to worry about as it was. I couldn't stay mad at Gran. I blamed God for all of it.

Three Left Turns

The air shimmered and twisted where it met the earth. The road beneath the tires of my bike was a ribbon of dust, hard-packed and hot, a backroad race-track, and I was gaining on him.

His BMX was kicking up a cloud of pretend motorcycle smoke. I smiled and pedalled through it, teeth grinding grit and lungs burning, because the stakes were so high.

If I won, I was faster, until next time, than my Uncle Jimmy. And if he lost, he was slower, until next time, than a girl.

Is the little brother of the woman who married your father's brother related to you? I called him my Uncle Jimmy, regardless, and he was my hero.

He was four years older and almost a foot taller than me, and I don't think I ever did beat him in a bicycle race, but the threat was always there.

Just allowing a girl into the race in the first place raises the possibility that one might be beaten by a girl, so the whole situation was risky to begin with. We all knew this, and I probably wouldn't have been allowed to tag along as much as I did had I been older, or taller, or a slightly faster pedaller.

Girls complicate everything, you see, even a girl like

me, who wasn't like most; you can't just pee anywhere in front of them, for instance, or let them see your bum under any circumstance, or your tears.

There were other considerations, too, precautions to be taken, rules to be observed when girls were around, some that I wasn't even privy to, because I was, after all, a girl myself.

It was the summer I turned six years old, and I was only beginning to see what trouble girls really were.

But I, it was allowed by most, *was* different, and could be trusted by Jimmy and his friends with certain classified knowledge. I was a good goalie and had my own jackknife, and could, on rare occasions, come in quite handy.

Like that day. That day I had a reason to tag along. I had been given a job to do, a job vital to the mission.

The mission was to kiss the twins. For Jimmy and his skinny friend Grant to kiss the twins.

The twins were eleven, and blonde, and from outside. Being from outside was a catch-all term used by people from the Yukon to describe people who were not from the Yukon, as in:

Well, you know how she's from outside and all, and always thought she was better than the rest of us, or, *I couldn't get the part and had to send it outside to get fixed, cost me a mint,* or, *well, he went outside that one winter and came back with his ear pierced, and I've wondered about him ever since.*

The twins were only there for the summer. Their dad was there to oversee the reopening of the copper mine.

They wore matching everything, and also had a little sister, who was seven.

That's where I came in.

The plan was a simple man's plan, in essence. As we worked out the details, we all stood straddling our bikes in a circle at the end of Black Street where the power line cut up the side of the clay cliffs.

We were all going to pedal over to where the twins and their little sister lived. We had already hidden the supplies in the alley behind their house. The supplies consisted of a small piece of plywood and a short piece of four-by-four fence post.

We would take the plywood and prop one end of it up with the four-by-four (Jimmy and I had two uncles who were carpenters, and he would himself go on to become a plumber) and build a jump for our bikes. Then we would ride and jump off it, right in front of the twins' house, which was conveniently located right across from the park (good cover). This would enchant the unsuspecting kissees-to-be (and most likely their little sister), drawing them out from their house and into the street, where they would be easier to kiss.

We would then gallantly offer the girls a ride on the handlebars of our bikes, having just proven our proficiency with bike trick skills by landing any number of cool jumps. The girls would get on our handlebars, and Jimmy and Grant would ride left down the alley with the twins, and I would take a right with their little sister and keep her occupied while they carried out the rest of the mission. The kiss-the-twins mission.

The only person more likely to tell on us than the girls, after all, was their little sister, and I had it covered. Keep her occupied. Don't tell her the plan. Don't wipe out and rip the knees out of her tights. Drive her around the block a couple of times, and drop her off. Grant and Jimmy would take care of the rest.

We thought we had pretty much everything covered. We even had secondary strategies; if the jump didn't work right away, we could always make it higher, and if that didn't work, I could bravely lie on the ground right in front of it, and they could jump over me.

It was a good plan, and it worked.

What we hadn't foreseen was, I guess, unforeseeable to us at the time. The girl factor, that is.

How could we have known that the twins' little sister would think that I was a boy?

And how had the girls already found out that Jimmy and Grant wanted to kiss them?

And what was I supposed to do if this girl, who was one year older than I was, slid off my handlebars as soon as we rounded the corner into the alley, planted both of her buckle-up shoes in the dust and both her hands on her hips, wanting me to kiss her like my uncle was kissing her older sister?

It hadn't crossed our minds, but that is exactly what she did (and I can't remember her name to this day, and so can't make one up, because this is a true story): the twins' little sister wanted me to kiss her, and I'm sure I must've wanted to oblige her, if only for the sake of the mission.

Because that is the first most secret, sacred tomboy rule: never chicken out of the mission.

There was only one problem. The girl problem. She didn't know I was one.

It wasn't that I had deliberately misled her, it just hadn't really come up yet.

And since me kissing anyone was never part of the plan as I knew it, I had not given much thought to the girl factor. But this girl had a plan of her own.

There she was, all puckered up and expectant-like, and it seemed to me I had a full-blown situation on my six-year-old hands.

A mistake had been made, somewhere, by someone. But what was it?

I had a number of options at that point, I guess.

I could have put my left hand on the back of her yellow dress, my right hand over her smaller left one, and given her a long, slow ...

No, I would have dropped my bike.

I could have leaned awkwardly over my handlebars and given her a short, sloppy one, and just hoped for the best, hoped that there wasn't something about kissing a girl the boys couldn't tell me, any slip that might reveal my true identity.

I might even have gotten away with it. Who knows? I would have liked for this story to have ended that way.

But it didn't. And because this is a true story, I would like to tell you what really went down with me and the twins' little sister in an alley by the clay cliffs the summer I turned six.

But I don't remember.

What I do recall was that unexplainable complications had arisen because we did not take the girl factor into consideration, rendering this mission impossible for me to carry out.

According to Grant and Jimmy, the little sister started to cry when the dust had cleared and she found herself alone, in an alley, in this weird little town where her dad made her come for the summer, and the twins had to take her home.

And when all three left, two weeks later, unkissed, Grant and Jimmy still considered me a major security risk.

But I don't remember my retreat.

My Aunt Norah was seventeen, and babysitting us that day. She said I came flying up the driveway, dumped my bike on her lawn, streaked past her into the living room, and threw myself on the couch, sobbing incoherently.

I would like to think that at this point she patted my head, or hugged me, or something, to calm me down, but we weren't really that kind of a family. It's not like I was bleeding or anything.

She said that when I finally calmed down enough for her to ask me what was wrong, all I could say was three words, over and over.

I don't know. I don't know. I don't know.

Girls. We can be so complicated.

My Hero

Webster's New School and Office Dictionary defines a hero as a man of distinguished courage, moral or physical; or the chief character in a play, novel, or poem.

Her name was Cathy Bulahouski, and she was, among other things, my Uncle John's girlfriend. She had other titles, too—my family is fond of nicknames and in-jokes—she was also referred to as the girl with the large glands, and later, when she left John and he had to pay her for half of the house they had built together, she became and was remembered by the men as "lump sum." The women just smiled, and always called her Cathy.

Cathy Bulahouski, the Polish cowgirl from Calgary. I've wanted to tell this story for years, but never have, because I couldn't think of a better name for a Polish cowgirl from Calgary than Cathy Bulahouski.

I remember sitting in her and John's half-built kitchen, the smell of sawdust all around us, watching her brush her hair. Her hair was light brown and not quite straight, and she usually wore it in a tight braid that hung like a whip between her shoulder blades. When she shook the braid out at night, her hair cascaded in shining ripples right down her back to just past the dips behind her knees.

She would get John to brush it out for her, she sitting

at one end of a plain wooden table, he standing behind her on their unpainted plywood floor. I would be mesmerized, watching her lean her head back, showing the tendons in her neck. Brushing hair seemed like a girl-type activity to me, but John would stroke her hair first with the brush, then smooth it with his other hand, like a pro. My father rarely touched my mother in front of me, and I couldn't take my eyes off this commonplace intimacy passing between them.

The summer I turned eleven, Cathy was working as a short-order cook at a lodge next to some hot springs. She was also the horse lady. She hired me to help her run a little trail ride operation for the tourists. My duties included feeding, brushing, and saddling up the eight or so horses we had. And the shoveling of shit. I wasn't paid any cash money, but I got to eat for free in the diner, and I got to ride Little Chief, half-Appaloosa and half-Shetland pony, silver grey with a spotted ass. Cathy and I were co-workers and con-spirators. Every time we got an obnoxious American guy she would wink at me over his shoulder while he drawled on about his riding days in Texas or Montana, and I would saddle up Steamboat for him, a giant jet black stallion who was famous both for his frightening bursts of uncontrol-lable galloping and for trying to rub his rider off by scraping his sides up against the spindly lodge-pole pines the trails were lined with.

I always rode behind my aunt; Little Chief was trained

to follow her horse. Hers would plod along at tourist speed in front of me, and I would try to make my legs copy the way hers moved, the seamless satin groove her hips fell into with every swing of the horse's step.

Sometimes we would ride alone and she would whistle and kick the insides of her boots in and race ahead of me. Little Chief would pick up the pace a bit like the foot soldier he was, and my heart would begin to pound. Cathy would ride for a while and then whirl her horse around, her long braid swinging, then hanging down her front as she rode back towards me.

One day we were lazily loping alongside the little road that led back to the hot springs when one of Cathy's admirers came up from behind in a pick-up. He honked hello as he and his road-dust drove by, which spooked Little Chief and he bucked me off.

On impact, tears and snot and all the air in my lungs were expelled. I lay on the hard-packed dirt and dry grass for a minute, bawling when I could catch little pieces of my breath.

"Get on," Cathy said, hard-lipped as she rode up beside me. "Get back up on that horse right now. Do it now or you'll be too afraid later."

She was tough like that.

One Christmas Eve shortly after she and John had finished drywalling, our family gathered to have turkey dinner out at their place. We were each allowed to open one present, and my mom had suggested I bring the one shaped just like a brand new toboggan from under our tree at home.

The coolest thing about Cathy was how she would gear up in a snowsuit in thirty below in the blue-black sky of a Yukon night (which begins at about two in the afternoon around solstice) and go play outside with the rest of the kids. Not in a grown-up, sit-on-the-porch-and-smoke-cigarettes-and-watch kind of way, but in a dirty-kneed, get-road-rash-kid kind of a way. Right after I ripped the last of the wrapping paper off my gleaming red sled, she was searching through the sea of snowboots by the door for her black Sorels and pulling her jacket off the hook behind the door.

"Let's go up the hill behind the house and give it a try. Not much of a trail in winter, but we'll make one."

I suited up right behind her, followed by my sister and a stream of cousins with mittens on strings.

It was so cold outside that the air burned arrows into the backs of our throats and frost collected on our eyelashes above where our scarves ended, which would melt if you closed your eyes for too long and freeze on your cheeks.

We packed as many of us onto the sled as we could so everyone could have a go. We rode and climbed, rode and climbed until our toes began to burn. "Once more, everybody goes one more time, then we should go in," Cathy breathed through her scarf. She pushed her butt to the very back of the sled, and motioned for my little sister to shove in front of her, between her legs. I jumped in the front, and my little sister's snowsuit whistled up against mine as she wrapped her legs around me. The toboggan's most alluring feature was the two metal emergency brakes on either side, with the black plastic handles molded to fit the shape of your hand. I tried to grab both and steer, but my sister also wanted to hold onto one, and started to whine. "You can each have one," Cathy ordered. "You steer one way and you can steer on the other side, okay you guys? Don't fight about it, everyone else is waiting for their turn. Let's go."

About halfway down we flew off a bump. My little sister hauled on her brake and we screeched off the path and smashed into a tree. Cathy's leg hit first and I heard a snap.

By the time we rolled her onto the sled and pulled her back to the house, her face was glowing blue white and her teeth were chattering. John came running out with a flashlight. He gingerly pulled up the leg of her snow pants and dropped it again, his face changing from Christmas rum red to moonlight white.

"Jesus Christ. Get the kids in the house and pull the truck around. And get her a blanket, she's going to emergency. Pat, are you okay to drive?"

A weird silence took over the house after they left. I fell asleep in my clothes on the spare bed and barely woke up when my dad carried me out to the truck hours later.

"Did Cathy live?" I whispered into his ear. He smelled like scotch and shampoo and his new sweater.

"She's fine. She's asleep. She's got a cast and a bottle of painkillers. You can call her in the morning."

I told my friend Valerie all about it the next day, bragging like it was me. "I tried to save us, but my sister is too little to steer. Cathy's bone was poking right out of her leg, and she never cried once. There was even blood. Now she has a little rubber thing on the bottom of her cast so she can walk a bit, plus she has crutches."

"My dad cut the tip of his finger off with a saw once. They sewed it back on," she reminded me.

"Yeah, but you weren't even born yet. Besides, a leg is way bigger than a finger. Hurts more."

Later that winter the wolves got hungry because the government sold too many moose hunting licenses, and dogs and cats started to disappear. Cathy phoned me one Sunday morning and told me that they had found what was left of Little Chief at the bottom of the mountain the day before.

"I didn't tell you yesterday because your mom told me you had a hockey game. I know you're sad, but horses and wolves are animals, and they follow different rules than we do. He had a good horse life, and now the wolves will make it until spring. You were too big to ride him any more anyway, and your little heart will get better in time. Wolves are wolves and men are just people."

She was tough like that.

When she left John, she was tough too. She took her horse and one duffle bag, and most of his savings to cover her half of the house. She never even cried. Or that's how I saw her leaving in my mind. Dry-eyed in her pick-up, with the radio on and a cloud of dirt-road dust from the Yukon straight back to Alberta.

Bet she never looked back, I thought.

My uncle started to date one of the other cooks from

the lodge. She had a university degree so everyone called her the professor.

My little sister grew up and moved to Calgary. She, like myself, inherited our family loyalty, and looked Cathy up.

My mom and I went to visit my sister at Christmas, and she told me Cathy would love it if I could make it out to visit her in Bragg Creek. But we got snowed in, so I called her the day before we left.

Cathy's voice sounded the same as I remembered, except more tired. "I can't believe you're almost thirty years old. I remember you as just a little girl with that white hair and filthy hands, little chicken legs. You had such big eyes. My God, you were cute. Just let me grab my smokes."

I could hear dogs barking and a man cursing at them to shut the hell up. A television droned in the background.

She sounded out of breath when she got back on the phone. "Here I am. Hard dragging myself around since my accident. Did Carrie tell you about my legs?"

She had broken both of her femurs straight through a couple of years ago, and had pins in her knees. She still had to walk on two canes and couldn't work any more.

"I lost the trailer," she explained. "Couldn't get worker's comp because it happened on a weekend, and the unemployment ran out a year ago. Had to move in with Edward and lie about being common-law even to get welfare."

"What are you saying about me?" I heard the man's voice again in the background. "Who you talking to anyway?"

"My niece. Turn down the TV, for chrissakes."

"You don't have any nieces. You don't even have any brothers or sisters."

I presumed this was Edward. He obviously didn't understand family loyalty the way we did. Blood and marriage were only part of it.

"'Member that time you broke your ankle on the sled? You didn't even cry. You were my hero back then, you know?"

"Well, I cried when I broke my legs this time. I'm still crying. Some fucking hero I am now, huh?"

I heard the empty in her voice and didn't know what to say. So I told her a story.

"Your old shed is still out behind John's, you know. Nobody ever goes in there. A couple of years ago John said I should go out and see if your leather tools were still out there. Might as well, since maybe I would use them, and so I did. It was like a time machine in there. Everything was still hanging where you left it.

"I took down your old bullwhip. It didn't really want to uncurl, but I played with it a little and it warmed up a bit. I took it outside into the corral and screwed around with it. On about the hundredth try or so, I got it to crack. I got so excited by how it jumps in your hand when you get the roll of the arm right that I hauled off and really let one rip. The end of the whip came whistling past my head, and just the tip of it clipped the back of my ear on the way by, and it dropped me right into the dirt. I was afraid to peel my hand from the side of my head to see if there was still an ear there. Hurt like fuck.

"But I thought of you and made myself try a bunch more

times until I got it to crack again, you know, so I wouldn't be too afraid next time. Like you would have done."

She was quiet for a while on the other end of the line. "You still have some imagination, kid. Always did. You gotta come visit me sometime. I'd love to see what you look like all grown up. I don't get into Calgary much any more, only when Edward feels like driving, which is never. You'd have to come out here. Carrie could give you directions."

I've been back to Southern Alberta twice since then, but never made it to Bragg Creek to see Cathy Bulahouski, the Polish cowgirl from Calgary. She can't ride any more, she told me, and I couldn't bear to ask her if she had cut off her hair.

Two: Family I Have

Objects in the Mirror

Last month I spent ten days at home in the Yukon doing research for a new project. I went through as many family photos as I could lay my hands on: sorting through the magic red bag of memorabilia my Aunt Roberta keeps in her basement and sifting through the gigantic mishmash of memories crammed into a box in my mother's guestroom closet. My Grandma Pat won the organization award; hers were some of the only photos actually placed in albums, and each album had a glossary of subjects and decades listed on the inside cover in her bold, confident script. I found a citation for drunk driving from the seventies for one of my uncles, not totally out of character for him, but it was issued at ten o'clock in the morning, which was impressive. I unfolded a stiff and stern letter written by the principal of my father's high school, which would later be my high school, explaining to his parents just why he was going to have to repeat grade ten. It wasn't for lack of intelligence, he made sure to point out. I found a lot of pictures of me as a kid. Way more than I remember anyone taking at the time.

There is the one of me with my dad and my Uncle Rob, who are on either end of a broomstick loaded down with lake trout; I am crouching underneath the fish between the two men, blood spattered up to my elbows, proudly holding up a string of grayling. Me in a campground somewhere up north, exploding out of the willows, carrying a giant log of firewood on my back. Me on the first day of grade one, in a line-up with all the other little girls on the block; all the neighbour girls and my little sister are in sparkly new dresses, their chubby knees scrubbed and squishing out of the tops of sparkling white knee socks. I, on the other hand, am wearing blue corduroys, black rubber boots with red-brown toes, and my Davy Crockett fringed buckskin jacket. Me, in my grade two class photo, front-toothless in a plaid shirt, pearly snaps done right up to my chin, sporting an Andy Gibbish shag do. Me smiling in full hockey gear, lined up with all of my teammates, the only girl in the boy's league.

None of this was surprising to me; I appear to be the same kid I remember being. What I couldn't believe, in retrospect, is that anyone in my family could have actually been surprised when I came out of the closet at eighteen. The evidence was everywhere, right from the start; how could anyone have missed it?

I decided to investigate.

I called up my Aunt Roberta first, because it was almost eight o'clock in the evening, and she goes to bed early. I asked her if she ever suspected that I was gay when I was little, if she ever wondered about the hockey and the buckskin jackets?

I heard the kitchen chair complain about being dragged across the linoleum, and she sat down.

"I know this sounds silly, but I always thought you were

just who you were. An amazing little strong personality. Thought you got it from your dad."

I asked her if Gran had ever said anything to her about me and the gay.

"Gran's gone to bed already, but I do remember her saying to me that you were exactly right. All you kids turned out to be exactly who God meant you to be. I mean, you can call her in the morning if you want to, but I know that's what she'll say."

My grandma Pat was good for an awesome quote, as usual.

"I never labeled you as anything. You were just boyish, and you did boyish things. Keep in mind that we didn't think like that back then, you see. Any knowledge of homosexuality I might have had would have gone back to Victorian times. All those novels. You probably skirted under my radar, because you weren't wearing hoop skirts and high button boots."

My mom swore she had no clue whatsoever. "My mind never went there. I just let you be what you wanted to be. Not very helpful, I guess. I'm sorry."

My Aunt Cathy echoed my mom. "I just thought you were a little brat because you refused to wear a dress to our wedding."

My Aunt Norah thought my sister and I were simply polar opposites, that was all. "Carrie was the prissy little girl, and you ... weren't. You were just your own little people. When you were in your teens I remember thinking ... knowing somehow that you weren't happy, that you seemed tense inside your own skin. I knew there was something going on with you, but I didn't know what it was. We didn't have to have a label for everything back then."

My Uncle John was cooking an omelet in the background when I talked to him. "Sorry, kiddo, but I can't identify the moment we realized you had gone to the dark side. We were just glad you weren't stupid. There's no cure for stupid. There was that one time, you were only six or so, when you gave me supreme shit for not attending to my fishing rod, but I don't think that had much to do with your sexuality."

My Uncle Rob was pensive, thinking over his response a bit before speaking. "Well ... you can see why we wouldn't have thought much about it. There's lots of hetero butch chicks out there, to be honest. Especially up here."

"On the other hand," he continued, "maybe a guy should have twigged due to your aversion to wearing a dress, but who cares, anyway? I've always said, it's your soap and your dick, and you can wash it as fast as you want."

So it appears that for all those years, in all those photographs of that little tomboy, there was only one member of my family wondering about me.

And that was me.

The Curse?

I called my cousin up the other day, and partway through our usual gab he informed me that Layla, his stepdaughter, had some very exciting news.

"Can I tell Ivan, or do you want to tell her yourself?" he asked her from his end of the living room couch.

I heard her almost teenage voice in the background, saying it was fine; he could go ahead and tell me.

"Layla got her period this morning." He sounded proud, like she had won the science fair, or got straight As, something along those lines.

I was unsure how I should respond, but they both sounded happy on their end of the phone, so I asked to speak to Layla directly.

"Congratulations," I told her. "It sounds like some sort of a celebration is in order. You have anything in mind?"

I couldn't help but think back to my big day. My mom was out of town at the time, and when I called my Dad upstairs to ask him what I should do, he panicked on the other side of the bathroom door, emptied out my mom's drawer in the other bathroom, whacked his toe on a doorjamb, swore profusely, and then tossed me a box of anal suppositories, mistaking them, I believe, for some sort of feminine hygiene product. Neither of us were proud of me, and we never mentioned the subject again.

"Can you take me to see *The Corpse Bride*?" Layla asked me. "And can we have popcorn?"

"That is an excellent plan," I told her. "I'll pick you up at 6:30. It's a date."

On my way over, I pondered whether or not I should discuss the merits of menstruation with my young friend. It was obvious that this was a brave new world, and that Layla was being brought up to believe that her period was not a dirty female secret like it was when I was twelve years old, and this was a good thing. But I wondered if it would be strange for her to chat about it all with her butch relatives, or if my silence on the matter would be noted.

"So, you got your period, huh?" I asked her as she did up her seatbelt.

She nodded casually.

"Cool," I said, feeling like a gigantic dork. "Way to go."

And that was the end of that.

A couple of days later, I got mine. I plodded through the slush on the sidewalks to the corner store for a box of tampons. I went up both aisles twice, and couldn't find them.

Finally the guy behind the counter asked me if I needed any help finding something.

Normally, I would just shake my head and grab a can of soup, so I didn't have to say the word tampon to the guy behind the counter at the corner store, but this was a brave new world. I needed to get with the times, and cast off my shame and embarrassment, for the sake of young girls everywhere.

"Uh, yeah, I'm looking for tampons," I said.

"For what?" There were two other guys waiting to buy their cigarettes, and they both looked at me.

"Tampons."

He shook his head again, and cupped one hand around his ear, signaling that he couldn't hear me, I needed to speak up. I considered my options. I could scream out in a crowded corner store that I needed a box of tampons, or I could run for the door.

I chose the door.

The next corner store had an ample supply, and I let out a huge breath I hadn't realized I had been holding in. I took the box up to the counter along with a couple of other items I didn't really need, for cover.

I don't know why I am uncomfortable saying the word tampon out loud, or acknowledging the fact that I, like almost all estrogen-based organisms my age, get my period. Maybe it is residual Catholicism; maybe it is because most corner store guys think I am a young man on a supply run for his girlfriend or mother. Or maybe I just don't like to talk tampons with strangers.

"What brand is the best?" The guy behind this counter held up my tampons for the entire world to take notice of.

"I beg your pardon?" I was hoping I hadn't heard him properly, that this was not happening to me.

"There are so many brands to choose from, and different sizes, too. I never know what I should order, so I ask my lady customers, which one is the best?"

There was another guy behind me in line now, holding

a box of Kraft dinner and a loaf of white bread. He raised an eyebrow.

I felt a sudden rivulet of sweat in my armpits. Running for yet another door at this juncture would send the message that tampons are, indeed, a shameful topic. This thoughtful merchant had come to me for help in serving the needs of women throughout the entire neighbourhood, and it would behoove me to behave accordingly.

I took a deep breath and spoke in a calm, confident tone. "Well, I would say that it is definitely a matter of personal choice, similar to choosing the right condom for the job. A variety of sizes would obviously be a good thing, as there are many sizes of ... vaginas out there."

He nodded and leaned forward, interested.

"And as for brand, I always prefer the ones without an applicator for, you know, environmental reasons, but again, I can only speak for my own ... I can only speak for myself. I guess as wide a variety as you can carry would be my answer."

He thanked me and rang in my purchases. "Will you be needing a bag today?"

I nodded, and stuffed my tampons in, out of sight for the walk home. "You gonna watch the hockey game tonight?"

He shook his head. "I don't follow the hockey. Myself, I like cricket."

I shrugged. The guy behind me shook his head and stepped up to the counter as I headed for the door.

"Cricket, hey?" He was still shaking his head. "Well, each to their own."

By Any Other Name

I learned most of what I know about being a man from my Uncle Rob. Uncle Rob has never let the fact that I was declared female at birth get in the way of our male bonding, and I've always loved him best for it.

Uncle Rob taught me how to fish, drive a standard, light a match off of my front tooth, and open a beer with a Bic lighter. He taught me how to make a fist, turn into a skid, light a fire, and shoot a gun. He passed on to me everything he has ever managed to learn about women, and all the Zippo tricks he has ever been shown. He taught me how to tell a story, and how to hold my liquor. All the important stuff. Some of the family reckon I look more like my Uncle Rob than I do my own father, and everyone agrees I look just like my dad.

Uncle Rob and Aunt Cathy flew to Vancouver last week, because Rob had an appointment with a fancy eye doctor. Whitehorse General Hospital is equipped to handle your basic medical tests and common ailments, but anything involving a specialist or an expensive machine requires a trip to the big city. Rob called me from the hotel and told me to round up the stray cousins and bring the girlfriend; he was taking us all out for dinner. Cousin Darryl's brand new baby had somehow turned into a seven-year-old girl, and I hadn't seen my cousin Garth since Grandma Pat came to town for her knee replacement three years ago. I rarely bring a date along to family functions, because more than two or three of us in one room can be hazardous, especially if you are shy, offend easily, are clean and sober, or don't eat meat. The way my family demonstrates our love and affection for each other has occasionally been mistaken for verbal abuse by outsiders, so I usually don't take the risk.

But I knew she could hold her own; she is smart and strong and can take a joke. She loves fishing and hates hippies. There was common ground, and she might just fit right in. Besides, I figured, how could she love me and not like my Uncle Rob? He was the man who taught me everything I knew, and I look just like him.

The appetizers arrived in the middle of a raucous debate about flatulence and love: was unabashed farting in front of the fairer sex an expression of intimacy, or the sign of the death of romance? Was pulling the covers over her head actually a form of foreplay? Was our whole family actually lactose intolerant, or did we just not chew our food enough?

My sweetheart was unfazed, and retained her appetite. Maybe she really was the perfect girl for me.

By the time our entrees arrived, the talk had turned to embarrassing stories from when I was a kid, how I had panic attacks when forced into a dress for weddings, and how I finally gave in and wore a satin gown with dyed-to-match pumps to my high school graduation, just like the normal girls did.

"She looked so pretty," said Aunt Cathy solemnly, like she was giving my eulogy.

"I looked like a drag queen."

Darryl shook his head. "I can't imagine cousin Ivan in a dress."

"I can't imagine calling her Ivan." Cathy stabbed a bit of broccoli with her fork. "She'll never be Ivan to me. That's just, like, your writing name, right? Nobody actually calls you Ivan in person, do they?"

Cathy asks me this, even though the entire table had been calling me Ivan all night. I stopped using my birth name over a decade ago, but Cathy likes to pretend she doesn't know this because it makes her uncomfortable. I love her enough to allow her this tiny corner of cozy denial, and my continued silence on the matter helps to hold up my half of her little charade.

I have lots of people who call me Ivan. I only have the one Aunt Cathy. She has never understood why I changed my name, or why I vote NDP. I've never understood why she collects Santa Claus dolls, or how she can smoke menthols. It doesn't mean we love each other any the less for it.

"I've always called Ivan Ivan," states cousin Darryl, God bless him. No wonder everyone thinks he's gay.

"Are we allowed to have dessert?" squeaks second cousin Rachael.

"Anybody want to try a prawn? Going, going, gone."

Rob speaks around a mouthful of his dinner.

"Don't chew and talk at the same time, Robert. You'll set a bad example. There are children present." Cathy half-feigns disgust and backhands her husband in the upper arm, right where his shirtsleeve stopped and his tanline started. This signaled the official change of subject.

"Set a bad example for little Rachael?" Rob smirks, rubbing his arm where she had whacked him one. "It's already too late for Rachael, too late for all of them. I saw it on the Learning Channel. A child's personality is fully formed by the time they turn three. We might as well relax and let it all hang loose. The kid is already who she's gonna be, all we can do now is love her. It's out of our hands."

Rob leans across the table to pinch one of my fries. "Did Garth tell you him and Allison are getting hitched in Fiji? Cath and I are going. You and your lovely lady friend should come too. I'll rent us a boat and we can go fishing. The wedding is still over a year away, so start saving up. Maybe even Darryl will have a girlfriend by then, and we'll all go. A family that fishes together stays together, isn't that what they say? And you two girls would love Fiji. It's the perfect place for you, really: it's beautiful there, and the policemen wear skirts."

To Whom it May Concern

I don't want to sound like someone's grandmother or anything here, but really, would it be so hard to pick up a phone
and call? You don't even have to call me, just call anyone,
your brother, your dad, any of us, just to let us know that
you are alive. We all talk, you see, hoping that one of us has
seen you, or heard word, or even heard a rumour.

I'm not even the worrying kind, you know me, I get
really busy too and forget to keep in touch and miss my
cousin's birthday or whatever, just like everyone else, and
I'm definitely not usually the type to get on anyone's case
for stuff like this. It's just that the last time I saw you, you
had lost about thirty-five pounds and the crystal meth was
starting to turn your back teeth black, and the newspapers
and the streets are full of stories about irreversible brain
damage and psych wards brimming with lost souls strick-
en by this addiction, and, well, I worry. It's not like you're
backpacking in Europe and just forgot to send a postcard.
I don't care about broken promises or the money you owe
anyone. I do care that your brother and your dad spent another Christmas wondering where you were, and that they
are running out of reasons you haven't seen your niece and
nephew. I can't help but care about that, but even that I
would let slide.

Some guy asked me for change outside of the bank to-day. He looked skinny and drawn and nervous, just like you did the last time I ran into you on the Drive, and for some unexplainable reason I felt like punching him. Instead I took a deep breath and asked him when was the last time he called his mother?

The self-help books and the twelve-step doctrines would probably feed me some line right now about how no one can really help you until you are ready to help yourself and to not to allow myself to feel hurt that I haven't heard from you in almost a year, that it is your addiction govern-ing your behaviour right now and not you. But I call bullshit on that. We have known each other since we were kids, I would and have done anything to help you, and I deserve better than this.

This not knowing. Remember when I dragged you off the street and let you sleep it off for days and fed you and helped you track down the bits and pieces of your life so you could start putting them back together? Back then you said you were done with it all, you were ready, you wanted to change your life, and you needed my help.

I told you that night on the back porch I would do what-ever it took, anything in my power to see you through this time, but that I had one condition. My one condition wasn't even that you stay clean, because I know what a demon the meth is, and I didn't want you tossing me out with the clean and sober bathwater if you backslid. My one condition was that you didn't lie to me anymore, that if you used I wanted to hear about it from you. No more bullshit.

Maybe that is why you haven't called, maybe the truth was something you thought I wouldn't want to hear, or something you weren't prepared to say out loud.

I asked after you at your favourite old coffee shop the other day. The owner's grandson, the cute one, he surprised me by saying yes, he had seen you, and that you were looking great, that you had cleaned up and were living in the suburbs somewhere, and working construction.

I let out the long breath with your name on it that I had been holding for almost a year, and went straight home to call your brother. I was so glad to have word that you were alive and well that it took me a couple of days to get around to wondering why you hadn't gotten in touch with anyone.

The guy who first said 'No news is good news' obviously never had a best friend fighting the ice.

And the guy who coined the phrase "fair-weather friend" never met either of us. I once told you I knew that if ever I found myself in your shoes, I had every faith you would be there for me, and you hugged me in place of a yes.

I think of you whenever I swim in a lake, whenever I pass a rusty pick-up truck on the highway, whenever I see the northern lights or a blue-eyed dog. I miss you whenever I hit my thumb with a hammer, ride my bike, or walk past a lawn that needs mowing.

I'm not writing this to judge you, or to make you feel guilty. I'm writing this to let you know that whenever you are ready, I will be here. I refuse to give up on you. The fire that burned my house down spared the garage, so I still have most of the tools you stored at my place. A couple of times I had to laugh out loud at the same time as I was cursing your name, as I've moved around a lot since my house burned down, and I must really love you, because I can't think of anyone else I would move an entire set of free weights five times for, myself included.

I will pick up that phone whether you are still using or not, and I will listen to you whether your news is rosy or rainy. I want you to know that I meant what I said on the back porch that night, no matter what. No bullshit. A lot of things have changed for both of us since then, but not my home phone number.

Oh yeah, and my grandmother says to say hello.

Single Malt

My dad used to be easy to shop for. Every Christmas and birthday, for as long as I can remember, I have got him a bottle of single malt scotch. What brand I chose changed yearly; it depended largely on my economic status come shopping time, but that was all okay by him. I knew in my leaner years that he could just pawn the cheaper stuff off on his visitors. I've caught him guiltlessly pouring an Oban for himself, back turned, while simultaneously serving his houseguests Johnnie Walker Red. I once caught him trying to pull this stunt on me, red-faced with a bottle of Canadian Club in his hand, as if he thought I wouldn't know the difference.

I reminded him I had been trained by a professional.

A couple of Christmases ago, my Uncle Rob trapped me coming out of the washroom to have words with me about this. "Why buy booze for a guy who drinks too much?" he asked me with rum and eggnog on his breath. "Why not get him socks or something, like everybody else does now?"

Rob had a point, to be sure, and it wasn't like I hadn't thought about it all. But my dad already owns every tool known to mankind, never wears ties, hates sports of any stripe, and only wears work shirts. The contents of his closet reveal a repeating pattern: GWG boot cut jeans, thirty three-inch waist, thirty three-inch leg. White Stanfield t-shirts, size medium. Blue BVDs, also medium. Tan work boots, size nine men's. Grey and white work socks, the kind with the red stripe. He reckons if you own all the same socks, you don't have to throw both away when you get a hole in one. Easier to sort that way, too. A couple of summers ago he got himself a pair of sandals, and the whole family almost fell over in collective shock. Buying him clothes as a gift would be like going out for supplies.

My dad throws stuff away when he knows he won't use it, even gifts. After a couple of Boxing Day heartbreaks when taking out his garbage, I settled myself into buying him something I was sure he would love, something I knew would never go to waste. Scotch it was.

Last spring my dad called me out of the blue, which should have been my first clue that something big was up. The second alarm bell went off when he asked me how my girlfriend was. Sure, he didn't know her name, but that was as much my fault as it was his: I had stopped telling him years ago. But still, he asked.

Then the bottom fell out of all things predictable. My father interrupted me, stopped himself, and went on to say the following: "I'm sorry, I interrupted you. What was that you were saying?"

I immediately called my grandmother to find out if he was okay. "Is my father dying of cancer or something? He's acting very weird. First of all, he called me up just to talk. Then, he apologized for interrupting me. Is everything alright?"

"Of course," she said, laughing her little laugh, letting air out through her nose like she does. "The new Don takes a little getting used to. Yesterday, he called to let me know he was going to be late for lunch. Very unusual, indeed. Usually he just wouldn't show up and then avoid me until he thought I'd forgotten. But everything is different since he quit drinking."

My mind reeled through the rest of our conversation. The details rolled around my head and only stuck later, because I had yet to fathom the first line. I heard her say he just got up and poured it all down the sink, that it had been over a month now, but I was still stuck on imagining my father without a drink in his hand and wondering what his voice might sound like, thin-tongued and without a tinkling soundscape of ice cubes behind it?

When I visited in July, he was clear-eyed and full of wisdom; simple, yet sublime. "I realized," he said to me, swirling black tea with one sugar and tinned milk, "that it looks like I'm probably going to have the same wife, the same job, the same house, and work on this same little piece of ground for the rest of my life." He paused to light a smoke with steady hands. "And that the only thing I could change was my attitude."

We drove around town, going to pick up sheets of aluminium, welding rods, one-inch square tubing, and two-inch fine thread bolts, talking the whole time. It was just like when I was a kid, the only difference being that my dad now would allow the proud-biceped kid who worked in the warehouse load the really heavy stuff into the back of his pick-up. "Better his spine than mine," he whispered to me out of the corner of his mouth by way of explanation. His hair was a streak of silver, so startling, I could never lose him in the aisles. He seemed shorter, somehow, than I remembered him.

He lit a smoke when we got back into the truck, letting it dangle from one corner of his bottom lip as he backed the truck up with one hand, his right arm draped over the back of the seat between us. He has always been able to do almost anything with a cigarette in his mouth like this. Somehow, the smoke never gets in his eyes. "You know what?" he asks, eyes on the road. "I used to drive downtown, just like this ... before."

"Before" is the term my dad uses. He will not say "when I was drinking." He does not use the word alcoholic. Everything is just before, or after. You have to just let him talk. He won't answer direct questions. I don't push him, I'm just so glad it's after now.

He continued, because I said nothing. "I used to drive around, and everything seemed like it was broken, or abandoned, or it needed a paint job. Nobody smiled. I really felt like it was hell right here on earth, some days." He cleared his throat. "But now, I come down here, like today with you, and all I see is new construction, heavy equipment, girls in tight shirts ... and a lot of chrome." He looked at me out of the corner of his eye, to register my comprehension. "You know, all the things I like."

After I got back, I was afraid to phone him all summer, afraid to hear that his voice had slowed and dropped, afraid he would let the phone ring and ring and I would know. Scared that things had changed, or worse, that they had gone back to being how I thought they always would be.

I called him last week; I had to finally, to see what he wanted for Christmas. He sounded fine, but the stone in my stomach didn't dissolve until I heard him laugh. He didn't laugh that much, before.

"Don't get me anything. I'm good. Don't you worry about me. Or, how 'bout you get me something we both know I'll like. How 'bout you get me a carton of smokes?"

Thicker than Water

Everybody always says I look just like him. Every once in a while, my grandmother hauls out the second oldest photo album from her closet and opens it on the kitchen table, next to the cut crystal bowl of sugar cubes and the matching cup that holds the little silver teaspoons. She slides the teapot aside to make room and squints over her bifocals. If I have brought a friend with me, this is the part where she makes them try to pick out which face in the faded black-and-white photos belongs to my father. My dad has three brothers. They are wearing matching plaid shirts, or bathing suits, or cub scout uniforms, or hand-me-down pajamas and holsters for their cap guns. In the background there is a Christmas tree, or a lopsided front porch, or a wall tent, or a brass statue of a war hero from the summer the old man took them to Winnipeg to see the army base and learn some respect for the soldiers who fought and died so the rest of us could sit around in our underwear and read comic books and not eat the peas or the broccoli he worked all day to pay good money for. It is always easy to find my dad's face in the photographs. I look just like him, but without the ears. My grandmother named him Don, after his father, she tells my friend. This is the part where if it is raining or her knees are bad she will confess that she never really loved the old bastard, that he was never half the man his sons turned out to be.

More and more, I find little bits of my father in me. Not just around the eyes or in the shape of my jaw, but how I can't stand to have less than half a tank of gas in my car, because you never know. How I hate cheap tools and dull knives and loose screws. How I own twenty pairs of the exact same underwear. How I can't stop looking for something until I find it, even when I'm late, even if I don't need it until the day after tomorrow. I have to know where it is. My smokes are always in my left pocket, lighter in the right. I can't sleep if the dishes aren't done, can't read only half of a book, and I never turn off the radio until the song is over. I like a little bit of egg, potato, and bacon in every bite of my breakfast. It is a finely tuned ratio, constantly being weighed and adjusted throughout the meal. Nothing worse than winding up with only hashbrowns in the end. Always let your engine warm up before you drive anywhere and cool down a bit before you turn it off. You can double the life of a motor if you treat it right. Driving fast burns more gas and is hard on your brake pads. Besides, you just spend more time waiting for the light to turn green. Don't go grocery shopping on an empty stomach. All of these things I learned from my father. Most of the time I do them without thinking of him, but every once in a while I remember; these are inherited habits. Other fathers might have saved their bacon until last, or ran out of gas, or hired someone else to build their house. Other fathers might have worn dress shoes to work instead of steel-toed boots. A different kind of dad might not have taught me how to weld. A man with sons might not have let his daughter drive the forklift. Who would I be if he had been someone else?

A couple of months ago, I had a gig in Calgary. An all-queer spoken word show at a sports bar downtown, right in the middle of the hockey playoffs. Strange, but true. I was wearing a dark blue shirt with thin stripes, and a sky blue tie that subtly highlighted the secondary tones of my shirt. The waitress liked my stories and kept slipping me free scotch on the rocks after the show, and I had about four stiff drinks in me when this huge guy in a Flames jersey grabbed me by the necktie and pulled my nose right into his chest hair.

"Your tie is all messed up. Where'd you learn that? Nobody ever taught you how to do a proper double Windsor? You're a disgrace. Come here, lemme show you."

I tried to explain that I had been drinking, and was thus unable to engage in activities that required concentration or hand-eye co-ordination, plus it was dark and my tie was fine anyway, but he pulled my substandard knot loose and laid a drunken death grip on my right shoulder.

"I'm in the Mafia. The Mafia knows how to tie a tie. You going to argue how to tie a tie with the Mafia, or you going to shut up and watch me do this right?"

I mentioned that I had read somewhere that the real Mafia never admits that there is a real Mafia, and that Calgary wasn't known for being a hotbed of organized crime, and that the odds were neither of us would remember any of this in the morning anyway, but he insisted. I ended up getting a nonconsensual thirty-minute lesson in proper manly attire from a guy with one leg of his track pants accidentally tucked into his white sweat sock. He started with the double Windsor knot demonstration and went on to sum up the billfold versus money clip conundrum for me. He was pontificating on the merits of French cuffs when his buddy interrupted to announce they were all leaving to go catch the peelers.

I woke early the next morning, dry-mouthed and blurry. I pulled a clean shirt and a different tie out of my suitcase and was amazed when my fingers remembered what tying a perfect double Windsor knot felt like. I don't remember who taught me the wrong way to tie a tie, but I know for sure it wasn't my dad. He never wears neckties. He taught me how to tie a boat to a dock, and a fishhook to a line. How to tie double bows in your bootlaces so they never come undone halfway down a ladder or get caught up in a conveyor belt or a lawnmower blade and end up costing you a toe. My father is a wise man. He taught me all the important knots. The double Windsor I learned from a wise guy.

Maiden Heart

I put this story together over the last ten or twelve years, and it is still full of holes. It is a true story in the same way that an old vase that is broken into pieces in the sink and glued back together holds water. Maybe, maybe not. But it is no less beautiful to look at. This is what I think I know.

On October 31, 1997, my father turned fifty years old. He and my mother had split up about two years earlier, and as far as any of us could tell, he was attempting to drink himself into an early grave.

As always, he never let all that booze get in the way of a solid day's work, so he was half in the bag and all the way inside a tanker he was welding on when the phone rang in the little office at the back of his shop. He hung his torch up on the ladder and climbed out to get the phone. It had been ringing all day. Big family and a big birthday. Big pain in the ass.

"Happy Birthday, Don." The woman's voice was husky, with a bit of a smoker's rattle.

"Um, thanks." He didn't know who she was, but he felt as though he should. Something in her voice told him he should recognize her. Not the sound of her voice, more like the way she weighted down her words, like they meant something.

They chatted a short while; how was he doing, did he feel old, that kind of thing. She cleared her throat, paused for a second.

"You don't even know who this is, do you?"

"Keep talking," he insisted, sitting up a little in his greasy rolling chair. "I'll figure it out any minute."

"I should hang up on you right now."

"No no no, don't. Don't hang up. I will never sleep again from wondering. Just give me a hint."

"You forgot our promise."

My father took a sharp breath, dropped the pencil he had been fiddling with onto his desk.

"Patsy?"

She didn't speak, but wasn't silent on the other end of the phone line; a small, animal-like noise escaped her throat by accident, and thirty years hung in the space between them for a long second.

He repeated her name, more sure this time. "Patsy Joseph?"

She nodded, but he couldn't hear her nod, so she swallowed and spoke. "Uh-huh. It's me. And you forgot our promise."

My dad tells me this story in his boat, in 2003. It is August. We are in the middle of Marsh Lake, trolling one of his sweet spots for lake trout.

Patsy Joseph was his very first real girlfriend, he tells me, and she was two years older than him. They had promised each other when she was seventeen and he was fifteen that they would call each other on their fiftieth birthdays, no matter where they were. He had forgotten hers, almost two years earlier. She hadn't. Hadn't forgotten him at all.

They started talking on the phone quite a bit, and soon it was every day. She had left Whitehorse when her father moved to Hope, outside of Vancouver. The two childhood sweethearts never wrote or talked on the phone, he was mostly working in the bush back then, and they lost track of each other. When Patsy came back in the summer of 1969 to look for him, she heard from one of her girlfriends that he had gotten one of the Daws girls pregnant, and that he was married, was building a house up in Porter Creek somewhere. Catholic girl, what else could he do but the right thing?

Patsy was devastated, and left town with a truck driver who told her she had pretty eyes. Ended up in Dawson Creek. Good a place as any. Got a job in an auto parts place, on account of how my dad always made her help him fix up his '53 Mercury Comet convertible and so she knew a little about cars. More than most women did back then anyway. So, she still worked at the auto parts place, yeah, thirty years later, and she still lived with the truck driver, only he didn't drive truck anymore, he was on disability because of his back and maybe he couldn't drive the long hauls like he used to, but he could still beat on her so they weren't really together, these last few years, she lived in the upstairs suite of their house and he lived on the ground floor, and she wanted to sell that house and be rid of him for good, but they couldn't, not with this market, and so there she was. She told my dad she still loved him, always had, that she

still had his old letters and birthday cards and some photographs. Kept them hidden from the truck driver all these
years. Jealous and mean, you know the type.

My dad and I share a weakness for a lady who needs
help. It feeds something big and empty in us to arrive on the
scene with a truck or jumper cables or a generator or wide
open kind of dumb heart; we like to think it sort of makes
up for always saying the wrong thing just when the song
ends and the room goes quiet. My dad told his childhood
sweetheart that he had not seen in over thirty years not to
say a word to her ex-trucker, just to pack up her car when
the guy was asleep, take only the stuff she really needed,
and drive to work like it was any other day, and he would
meet her there. He would take care of the rest. He would
take care of everything. He would take care of her. And did
she have snow tires?

The next bit of this story I heard much later, not in my
dad's boat, but in his 1981 Ford F-150 pickup truck, driving in a full-on blizzard on our way back from spending
the night in the little house in Atlin that he was building
for when he and Pat finally retired. They had been married
for about ten years. The windshield wipers thump-thumped
in the quiet but merciless storm; snow devils swirled on
the black ice in front of the two stab marks our headlights
made into all that oblivion. Nobody but us crazy enough to
be out on that road in this weather. Used to be when I was a
kid I was never scared when my dad was driving, no matter
how big the waves or black the ice. Now I am older. I light
his smokes for him so he doesn't have to take his hands off

the wheel for long. No streetlights here, just dark and snow and cold all around us, not even a light on in a cabin, not out here, not until we hit the main highway. His face is lit up only a little from the dashboard lights, and the cherry on his cigarette dangles in the dark when he talks.

He tells me how he drove almost all the way through the night, when he went south to go get her, and walked into the auto parts place in Dawson Creek in the early afternoon. She was behind the counter wearing an angora sweater, kind of light blue he thinks it was, and he tried not to let his face show it, but he couldn't believe how old she looked. She said it was time for her coffee break; did he want to come up to the lunchroom with her then? She wouldn't meet his eyes with hers, wouldn't look at him right on at all, kept hiding her face behind her bangs, which were still blonde, but shot all through with silver now. She told him much later she couldn't rest her eyes right on his face at all that day, not even for a second, because she couldn't believe how old he looked. Couldn't look right at the years in his eyes and stamped all over his face. So she stared out the window into the parking lot of the auto parts place even though there was nothing much to look at out there and she had seen it all a million times anyways, but it was better than turning around and seeing your beautiful memory grown old and wrinkled and grey and with a bit of a gut now. And my dad, he has never been any good at knowing the right thing to say, so he tells a joke. And she smiles at the joke, because he's funny, he really is, the old man is, and she turns to look at him just a little and then she laughs.

Light me another smoke, he tells me, and so I do, trying not to get any smoke in me at all because I quit for over a year now, which makes him not trust me in a way that neither of us can put our finger on.

"Anyway," he says, "that's when I saw her. The girl I fell in love with when I was a kid. She laughed, and all those years just fell away somehow, and suddenly it was just her and I standing there, together. So she quit her job and followed me home back to Whitehorse in her Lincoln Continental and I married her up at Nolan's reindeer farm with only an eight-fingered farm hand as a witness. Filthy old Danny Nolan is a justice of the peace, can you believe that? Didn't invite any of the family. Not even my brothers. John still hasn't forgiven me."

My father's eyes are shining with tears he will not allow to slip out and down his cheeks. He opens his window a crack and the wind sucks his cigarette butt out of his square-nailed fingertips and disappears with it. It was true. I had seen it for myself, the previous summer. I had seen Pat's face crack when she laughed and reassemble for a split second into a much younger memory of itself. Almost pretty. I can't even remember what the joke was, but I remember that face, remember wondering where it had come from, and where she hid it the rest of the time.

We finally make it to Whitehorse; the last fifty clicks into town we just trailed behind the snowplow, the storm swirling behind us and filling in our tracks as soon as we were gone. Pat has the coffee on, and all six of their dogs explode in a fit of barking when we stomp through the front door and strip off our wet parkas and heavy boots. Pat is pissed off, she is not saying anything but you can see it in her face. We shouldn't have been driving in that weather, and we both know it, so we say nothing.

I sit down at the little kitchen table and pour a dollop of evaporated milk into my coffee, add a sugar cube from the Roger's box on the counter. My dad is stoking the fire. The television is on but turned down so you almost can't hear it. She won't let him smoke in the house anymore, and it smells like the cinnamon-scented candle burning on the coffee table. There are several pictures that hang on the wall next to the bathroom, above the washer and dryer, right next to her Elvis clock. Pictures of the dogs when they were puppies, stuff like that. There is one of her and my dad, one she kept secret from her ex-trucker somehow, all of those awful years. She has had it blown up and framed. Black and white, my dad and her, back in the mid-sixties, he with his hair slicked back and his smoke pack tucked into the rolled up sleeve of his white crew neck t-shirt, his jeans with wide cuffs and his lips curled in a smile around his cigarette. She has a kind of beehive hairdo, and his arm is around her waist. They are standing in front of an old wall tent, and the chrome on the grill of the Mercury Comet winks in the sunlight beside them, and the soft shape of the mountain next to the Fox Lake campground rolls in the far background. The photo looks like something out of an old ad from *Life* magazine or something. This photo hangs right next to another one, this one in colour, a shot of the two of them again, her with her new perm and him with his silver shock of hair sticking up all over. He is wearing sandals and a clean work shirt with the sleeves pulled up over the welding scars on his forearms, and they are standing next to the Lincoln Continental, which is parked beside the motor home he traded a guy for some welding a couple of summers ago. In the background is the same mountain; they have returned to the very same campground site, it looks like, right there on the gravel beach of Fox Lake. But there was a forest fire there a couple of years ago, and so the trees left standing on the familiar shape of the mountain are crooked little blackened matchsticks, the fireweed curling up between them and taking over. My dad has a gut and his wife is squinting into the sunlight, her glasses catching a glint so you can't really see her eyes behind them. But none of this matters, really, because it is forty years later, and they are both smiling.

All about Herman

My grandmother has kept a journal for most of her life. All ninety years of it. She loves to write, she tells me on the phone from the Yukon. I can picture her, all the way from Vancouver, it is January, so she has the propane fireplace on in the living room and she is sitting with her legs tucked up beside her on the couch like she does. She is wearing a dress with a floral pattern and the rug needs a good vacuum, which she would do if she could still see the dirt, but she can't. There is the smell of drip coffee and bread dough set aside under a clean tea towel to rise. Newspapers and magazines cover the coffee table, and she has a fresh cup of black tea with cream and sugar in it on the side table, next to a plate empty save for a scattering of toast crumbs. She has lived in this little house on Elm Street in Whitehorse since 1967. It is the only house belonging to anyone in my giant family that has been there all of my life. Everyone else has sold and moved up, to make room for more kids, and later, less room for fewer kids. Only this house remains, as unchanged as playground concrete in all of our memories. I can't imagine my grandmother anywhere else but in this house, and I refuse to think about anyone else ever living here when she is gone.

"Did you get my envelope?" she asks me, as always

speaking far too loud into the receiver, as though she doesn't quite trust in the technology. "I sent you a copy of all of my latest scribblings."

She has been going back through her old journals, editing them and typing them up. Her vignettes, as she calls them. She has been sending me envelopes, sometimes containing carefully folded, ten-page-long stories handwritten in her sloping but still solid script, sometimes typewritten in all capital letters, with capital Xs crossing out mistakes, and corrections made in blue pen in the margins. Most are untitled, with just that day's date in the upper right hand corner. I read and re-read them; they are full of old stories, confessions, and advice. Lately her musings have grown somehow more poignant, more emotional, full of regrets.

"What I bitterly regret are the things I didn't say, and the questions I didn't ask," she writes. "I have dreams now, and I dream of the past. I am not old. I'm not an old lady. I am young, vibrant, full of life. I'm like that in all my dreams. So I enjoy my dreams."

Her last letter was four pages long, typewritten. She has titled this one, called it "All about Herman." I don't remember Herman, as a child I knew of him only through escaped bits of stories whispered here and there, nobody talked about Herman much. He died Christmas Day in 1970; I never knew why. I knew next to nothing of the story of Herman until just last year, when my grandmother writes:

"It all started with the morning of March the 9th, 2008. It was his birthday on March the 9th, 1930. He has been dead now for thirty-eight years, and on this morning,

I am thinking about him. I remember him, and a week or so later, I can't get him out of my mind."

Herman had been an engineer for the Department of Public Works, and my grandmother was a secretary. She was married; her husband and three of my uncles had recently left the Yukon and travelled ahead of her to New Zealand, where she was to join them in a year, when they had found work and set up a place for them all to live. My dad didn't want to leave the Yukon; he was already working, driving a caterpillar in the bush on a road building crew. My grandmother was to stay behind and save all the money from her government job. At least that was the plan. But that is only sort of what happened.

It turned out Patricia liked being alone. This was unforeseen.

And then the big, rugged engineer began to court her. At first she turned him down. Finally, she agreed to go for a drink with him one night. They began an illicit affair. He took her on trips. He liked classical music. He was well-read. He was in love. And she was in trouble.

Time did what it does, and the day came for her to travel to New Zealand and be reunited with her husband and sons. Herman travelled with her to Vancouver, and put her on a steamship. When she arrived at the little cabin she was to share with two other women for the journey, it was full of flowers Herman had sent her. Her cabin mates thought she was crazy to leave a man like that behind.

"I haven't any words to describe my disappointment when I arrived in Auckland. The boat docked, and there he was. This husband of twenty-odd years that I was committed to spend the rest of my life with. He was there. He takes me home to a rented house, full of furniture bought on the hire-purchase, which I am supposed to get a job right away and pay off. He doesn't say I'm so glad you're here, welcome, I hope I can make you happy. He doesn't say any of those things. He just spreads the newspaper out on the table to look for jobs. For me. I do get a job. I am hired as office manager, switchboard operator, and tea lady. One of the mistakes I made was I used day-old milk; I also bought lemons when there was a lemon tree out in the yard, where I could have picked a lemon. Well, I had picked a lemon, twenty years ago.

"This was not a new life—just more of the same dismal, unhappy existence. Don, the man I had married, was not my friend. I began to dislike him, and that dislike eventually turned into hate. I had brought all of this onto myself. All right, I had allowed myself to have feelings for another man. How was I going to deal with that? Well, he dealt with it."

She eventually left Don and New Zealand, and returned to the Yukon alone. Her youngest son, John, would follow her in a year.

She tells me this part of the story forty years later, at her kitchen table, the part about how she pulled her car over to the side of the road in Cache Creek, at the crossroads, and pondered all those road signs for a long minute. Should she go back to the prairies, and her mother, or was it north she wanted? She claims she wasn't thinking of Herman so much in that moment. She tells me she thought it was over, that they had ended it. But she continued north, so I don't know if I believe her. I don't think it was me she was lying to. I'm no shrink, but I know enough to know when a woman most needs to believe her own lies first.

I get the story from her in snapshots, short bursts, late-night kitchen table talk when the lips are loose with the whiskey. I knew she returned to the north, it was why we were all still here. She tells me part of the story in 2004: she breathes out in one long sentence that my grandfather broke her nose in New Zealand. Just a detail, an aside in another story about something else. She doesn't rest on the memory, and I will myself not to react, so she won't lose her train of thought. She does that now, more and more. Yesterday on the phone she confesses that she never wrote to me much about what happened to her in New Zealand because she hates to remember it, wants her sons to hold a different past in their heads. A different father. My grandfather, and what he did.

"In a fit of pent-up bottled rage, he attacked me. I can't imagine his hatred, and anger that he would smash me in the face over and over again with his fist. The blood was spattered all over the wallpaper. He wanted to mess up my face, so that I wouldn't be attractive to another man. The kids were there, they knew what was going on. They saw it. They had to clean up the mess. Years later I asked Rob, I said what did you do about all that blood on the wall? He said, we cleaned it up."

Pat returned to Whitehorse, alone, and got herself a

job. She stayed with friends of the family and made no attempt to contact Herman. But they ran into each other on Main Street.

"He must have thought he'd seen a ghost," she writes. "We didn't speak very much, but he didn't go away. He came back. He came to see me. This time this was serious. We resumed what we had started. I thought our relationship was private. I thought nobody knew. I thought it was a secret. I thought we were kinda sneaking. It was not private. Everybody knew. The whole town knew. I didn't have to make a secret of it anymore. I was acknowledged as his partner, and I started divorce proceedings.

"I realize now the seriousness of his drinking problem. Like he was two people. Dr Jekyll and Mr Hyde. The Dr Jekyll was a good natured, amiable, agreeable, softhearted, generous, loving ... what else can I say? But the Mr Hyde could be terrifying. He could charge at me like an enraged bull, and he was bigger, he was twice the size of me. He wasn't fat, he was just meaty. I probably should have been afraid of him, but I wasn't. Because I knew he wouldn't hurt me. The last thing in the world he would do would be to hurt me.

"He built that house, and I know he built it for me, I know he did. We tried to live in it, but it just didn't work. There was just too much. It was battle stations all the time. I know it was the drinking. He spent a lot of time in bars. The Capital Hotel. I was not allowed to go there, and I never went there with him.

"He talked of getting married, but this bothered me. I

couldn't see that. But he told me that if I married him, he would give me a sapphire ring that would flash blue like my eyes did when I was mad at him. If that's a proposal, then I guess that's what it was.

"But it ended on Christmas Day, 1970. He collapsed in my house. Right there. Right there on the floor. A big, vital, alive man came crashing to the floor. I called the ambulance. In those days you didn't go with the ambulance, that wasn't done, you were in the way if you did. So I just hid in my second bedroom, I couldn't bear even seeing them taking him away. I didn't visit him until the next day. I went in there and I discovered that he had tried to walk out of the hospital. He had torn out his tubes and whatever they attach to you and tried to walk out. I thought this was probably a good sign that maybe he was going to be all right. Even when somebody said to me how's Herman doing? I said I think he's out of the woods. I said that. He was anything but out of the woods.

"That night I got the call about three o'clock in the morning that he had died. He was forty. Forty years old. The same age as you?

"But had he lived, he would be eighty-one today. He'd probably be as mean as sin. In a way, I am glad he never lived to see me grow old. I'm glad in a way. Because he wouldn't have been very nice about it. He would have been cruel. All in all, we were together about five years. I was as happy as I've ever been in my life.

"Which brings me back to March, 2008. I feel his presence. I don't believe in spirits. I can't imagine him going to heaven. He just wouldn't fit in. And the thought of me having to spend eternity with him in heaven? I'd rather not. We would just fight.

"You should only marry for two reasons. Only two reasons. Love or money. I know what real love is now. And what I had for Herman, there was nothing like it before him, nor has there been since. Passion helps. I mean it helps. It's the glue that holds the love together. Well, all right, sex. Let's face it. My love affair with Herman was passionate. Even when we fought, it was passionate. I think it can actually outlive death, and even time. In retrospect, I believe this. Now, I am ninety. Like sweet ninety and never been kissed? I still feel the same way about him that I did forty years ago. Believe it or not, that is the truth. He told me he liked to hold my little hand. Somehow, I'd like to think he still does."

Just a Love Story

A couple of years ago I was crammed into a Honda Civic hatchback with four poets, squinting through the furious wiper blades to find the right exit off of the Number One Highway into Surrey. We were on our way to a suburban high school for a gig.

The slam poet in the back seat with the relentless bad breath squeezed his face into the front seat. "It's Valentine's Day tomorrow. I think we should all do love poems."

There was an exuberant round of agreement from everyone but me. I cracked the passenger window just a little, and an icy spray of February rain hit my cheek. I took a deep breath and rolled the window back up. I was the only storyteller in the car. I am used to this. Used to being lumped in with the poets. This doesn't bother me. I have even stopped telling people I have never written a poem in my entire life. Storyteller, poet, close enough, I guess, for most people. Even though they are not the same thing at all.

"I can't read a love story in a high school in Surrey," I blurt out, feeling a bit like a parent who just busted in on a pillow fight.

"Why not?" the slam poet heavy-breathed from the back seat, his eyebrow raised in a question mark.

I was also the only queer person in the car. I am used

to this. This almost never bothers me. Gay person, straight person, what is the difference anymore, right? Aren't we over all that?

Truth is, I have been over it for decades now. Most of us mostly are. But not in a high school. And not here in Surrey, British Columbia. Surrey, where they banned the *Harry Potter* books from school libraries for encouraging witchcraft. They also banned *Heather Has Two Mommies* and *One Dad, Two Dads, Brown Dad, Blue Dads* for promoting anti-family values.

"Because," I say, letting out a long breath, "it is scary enough to be a homo in a high school in Surrey in the first place."

His face shows no sign of recognition, of understanding, of camaraderie, and I suddenly feel in-my-bones tired.

I take another heavy breath. "For you, a love poem is just that. A love poem. And I am glad for you, I truly am. But for me to read a love poem in a high school in the bible belt is a political statement, whether I mean it to be or not, someone will think I am recruiting, armpits will grow moist with tension, I will be pushing the homosexual agenda on unsuspecting adolescents, I will be disrespecting someone's interpretation of the words of their God, you know, the whole tired routine."

"So what?" pipes up the anarchist beat poet who had been slumped in the backseat beside the slam poet. "We've got your back, Coyote, fuck them all, rock the boat. Surrey needs it."

"What if I just want to tell a love story?" I asked. Only the thump of the windshield wipers responded.

I met her the first time eight years ago, in the hospital-ity room of the Granville Island Hotel, during the Vancou-ver International Writers' Festival. She was wearing tall red boots and her wool jacket and handbag matched. Silver and black ringlets surrounded her dimples and sparkling smart eyes. Some people you can see how brilliant they are from a distance, like there are little invisible sparks coming out of their brain while it is working, creating static electric charges in the air above their heads. She was electric spark smart, and all I remember is I could make her laugh. Every time she laughed, my heart pounded possibility. When I saw her from across the room, she kind of shone. Like God Himself was pointing her out to me with a glowing finger. I left with too many plastic glasses of free wine in my belly, and without her phone number in my pocket.

I ran into her on the Drive a couple of days later, just like I knew I would.

It was one of those early spring days in Vancouver, where all of a sudden the grey of the previous week gives way and suddenly it is raining cherry blossoms everywhere, a crushed and scented carpet of them underfoot. We were talking about music. Somehow the band Nirvana came up, I can't remember why, I like them all right, maybe they re-minded me of some other band I liked better, I can't re-member, but she told me that the album *Nevermind* was her favorite all-time record when she was in grade seven. I quickly did some silent math in my head. How could the sexiest, smartest, silver-hairedest woman I had ever met be too young for me to go out with?

"Grade seven?" I blurted out. "How can you be twenty-three? How did I get to be ... if I had met you in 1991 when *Nevermind* first came out, you would have been ..." I shuddered.

"Twelve years old." She laughed again. Like this didn't matter at all. "It's the grey hair, right? That fooled you? I started going grey when I was sixteen. Runs in the family." My shoulders seemed too heavy to hold up all of a sudden. I told her I was too old for her. She told me that age doesn't matter. I told her the only people who think there is no such thing as too old for you are usually too young to know any better. She told me that she had just come out of the closet, that she wanted an older lover. She told me I was being ageist. I told her I used to think people were just being ageist too, when I was her age. She told me I was being ageist. I told her I know. Then I let out a long sigh. Did what I had to do. Told her that I was a dirty rotten rotter, that I had been around the block a million times, that I had slept with more women than ... that I had slept with a fair number of women in my long and lucky life of loving, and that she should pick someone special, that this was her second chance at having a first time, and most people never get a second first-time chance at anything, that she was lucky, and not to waste that chance on a pussy crook like me. Go, I told her, and fall in love with a nice woman. Fall in crazy stupid dumb-struck love and move in together and figure yourself out, don't get a cat, though, and then fall out of love, suffer through a hopefully short but nevertheless nether-region-numbing bout of lesbian bed death, and break up. Lather, rinse, and repeat. I told her that if she still wanted me five years from now, to come and find me. I told her that if she still wanted me then, that I would be honoured. Told her I had to go, before I changed my mind. I would see her around from time to time. Usually at poetry readings. Started going to a lot of poetry readings. Started dressing up to go to poetry readings. Started ironing my shirts to go to poetry readings.

Five years later I am in my car, waiting to turn left off of Commercial Drive onto First Avenue, on my way to the Home Depot. My girlfriend and I have recently broken up. We still live together, which could have been awkward, but luckily she was often in Portland with her new lover, who made more money than me, had a really hot truck, and a brand new Harley. So of course I was doing what any self-respecting butch does in this kind of situation: I was throwing myself heart-first into a complicated home improvement endeavour.

This next part seems like magic, but it is true. Some would say this is evidence that magic is for real. I was listening to classic rock and Fleetwood Mac was singing about don't stop thinking about tomorrow, and so I was thinking about tomorrow, about how maybe this breakup was for the best anyway, right, because look, I was finally going to get the new floor down in my office, and wasn't I now free to do what I wanted with whomever I wanted, plus, hadn't it been five years now, so couldn't I take that silver fox out on a date now? Thirty-eight and twenty-eight wasn't so bad, right?

And that's when I saw her. Standing on the corner with

a coffee in her hand. Her hair now more silver than black, somehow even more beautiful. She waved when she saw me. I unlocked the passenger side door and she jumped in.

"Where you going?" she smiled, showing her one crooked tooth.

"Home Depot," I told her.

"I love Home Depot," she said, and winked.

We didn't get out of bed for three days. She did a lot of yoga, it turned out. I vowed to quit smoking, so I could keep up with her. Eventually, I did. Quit smoking, that is.

Last month we went home to the Yukon. My family loves her, especially my mother. I think she is actually the daughter my mother always wanted. She is so smart and dresses so fine and almost has her PhD and it almost makes up for my mom having me and my even blacker sheep sister as her real children.

I drove her out to one of my favorite places in the world, the Carcross Desert. White sand and mountains and so much sky all over the sky. Some dirt bikers had accidentally burned a huge heart shape into the sand with their back tires. We stood together in the centre of that accidental heart, and it seemed like the perfect spot to put that big old diamond ring on her finger.

My family is beside themselves. At dinner, my cousin Dan insists that I tell his sister the whole story of how we met. It's so romantic, he says. It is just such a love story.

The Rest of Us

I got the call on a Sunday night. My gran was in the hospital, and the doctor had advised the family that it was time. Time to call everybody home.

I arrived bleary-eyed at the Whitehorse airport the next day. My mom and Aunt Nora were both there to meet me and my cousin Robert and his girlfriend. They looked so tired and worried; the skeleton was showing behind their faces, their eyes red-rimmed and puffy. They took us directly to the hospital, our suitcases stowed away in the trunk of the car.

I knew my gran wasn't going to look good, and I thought I had steeled myself for the worst. Still, my heart stopped and dropped when I laid my eyes on the tiny shape of her, the outline of her hips and legs barely visible under the green sheets and blanket. Impossibly frail and little. Almost gone already, it seemed. I had promised myself I would be strong for my mom, that I wasn't going to cry. So much for that.

"Talk to her," my Uncle Dave said, waving two fingers at Robert and me. "The nurses say she can still hear us."

And so we did. All afternoon we sat and talked. To her, to each other. Remember her bad cooking? Baloney roast? Boiled hamburger? Lemon hard cake, cousin Dan had dubbed her attempt at meringue. How she loved us all, no matter who we were, no matter what we did. I volunteered for night shift, and sat next to the laboured breathing shape of her with my two uncles, whispering stories through the dark to each other, into her ear, slipping our warm hands under the covers to grasp her limp, cold ones.

By early the next afternoon all of us were there. Five of her children, eight grandchildren, plus partners. I began to worry that we were pissing the nursing staff off a little, them trying to work around us, asking us to leave the room so they could change her sheets. Ten or fifteen of us at a time, filing like exhausted soldiers out into the hallway to stand around, teary-eyed and sometimes bickering. I asked one of the nurses if we were driving anyone nuts yet, wasn't it hard trying to do her job with the whole lot of us underfoot? She shook her head and said no, that the First Nations people had taught the nursing staff what an extended family could really look like, and that it is often easier when the family is there to help keep an eye on a patient. She said that what was really hard was when someone was dying without anyone there at all. This choked me up a little, and she shoved a no-name box of Kleenex across the counter at me with a latex-gloved hand. She had said it out loud. The doctor was kind, and had talked around it. Don't get your hopes up, she had said. We are keeping her comfortable, the doctor said. The doctor didn't lie, but it was the nurse who actually said the words. My grandmother was dying.

Florence Amelia Mary Lawless Daws passed away a little after eleven a.m. on May 13, surrounded by seventeen members of her family. Our hands made a circle, all touching her tiny body as her chest rose and fell, and then stopped. I hesitate to say her death was beautiful, because it means I have to miss her now, but it was.

My family asked me to write and read her eulogy. Blessing from the family, the Catholics now call it. I call it what it is. Of course I said yes, I would be honoured, and I was.

I wrote about the values the tiny little Cockney/Irish/Roma woman had lived and died by, and raised us all up to believe in. Love your family, work hard, save your money, have faith, and be grateful for what you have. I worked really hard on the eulogy. I wanted to do justice to her memory, to honour everything she was. There were over four hundred people at the service, and not a dry eye among them when I was finished.

Up at the graveyard, after the internment, I hugged strangers and shook hands. Suddenly I found myself surrounded by Catholic priests. They were being uncommonly nice to me, the queer granddaughter in the shirt and tie. Maybe they make special allowances in the case of a death in the family, I thought. Or maybe they were still hoping to save my soul. The bishop hugged me, and then held both of my hands in his too-soft ones.

"Excellent job, young man. Your grandmother would have been very proud of you today, son. Strong work, young fellow."

My mother heard him too. I saw her freeze. Waiting.

"Thank you, Father," I said. That was why he seemed to like me so much. He didn't know who I really was.

The bishop caught up with me again at the reception, back at the funeral home. We were both leaned over the cheese platters, when he addressed me a second time.

"Once again, I must say, you are a gifted orator. A natural, even. Have you ever considered the priesthood?"

This time it was my Aunt Nora within direct earshot, and she stopped in mid-bite, half a baby carrot removed from her mouth and dropped on a small paper plate. Her eyes met mine, and she tried not to wince.

I took a deep breath. Thought about my beloved gran, about how much she loved the Church, and respected the bishop. He seemed like a nice enough guy.

I'm not going to lie and say that one hundred wise-ass quips didn't run through my head and gather on my tongue. They did. But what counts is what I actually said.

"No, Father, I have to admit, I have never considered the priesthood. But thank you again for the compliment."

The bishop nodded, and everyone around us relaxed and resumed eating and talking.

I like to think my gran would have been real proud of me.

Three: that Boy

Red Sock Circle Dance

August, 1974 † Whitehorse, Yukon
Five years old at the Quanlin Mall, Saturday shopping, and I was holding open the swing door for my mom and the cart. I remember I had half a cinnamon candy stick in my mouth and a red baseball hat with the plastic thing in the back pushed through a hole that was smaller than the smallest hole in the strap, a hole I had to make myself with the tip of a heated bobby pin.

So the rest of the strap stuck oddly out from one side of the back of my head, but I didn't care, because it was my Snap-On-Tools hat that my dad had given me, just handed it right over to me when the guy at the tool place gave it to him, he was buying rivets or concrete pins or something, and the hat said Northern Explosives too, in black block letters in an arch over the hole in the back part, and come to think of it, what I wouldn't do now for that hat.

So enough about the hat, this American tourist sees me holding the door open, and of course he assumes it's for him, so he won't bump his cameras together pushing past his belly to open it for himself, and he steps through the door, right in front of my mom and her groceries.

He thanks me down his nose in heavy Texan "Thank you, son," and sucks more fresh Yukon air through his teeth. He is about to speak to me again, to meet the people, to engage in a little local colour, in the form of a polite little boy, and perhaps, via a patronizing conversation with him, get to meet his lovely young mother, too, who also had my little sister in tow, perpetual snot on her upper lip, even in summer like this.

My mom interrupts this quaint northern moment, pushing the puffed wheat, two percent, and pork chop-laden cart briskly through the door. "She is not your son," she shoots out the side of her mouth and the door slams shut behind the surprised Texan. I can't see him anymore, there is just myself reflected in the dusty glass, and the back of my mom smaller in the background, as she pushed the cart and dragged my little sister to my dad's Chevy, where he was smoking behind the wheel.

We could hate the tourists a lot more back then, before the mines all shut down.

The pavement was so hot in the parking lot that the bottoms of my sneakers stuck to the tar that patched the cracks on the way back to my Dad's truck.

April, 1992 † Vancouver, B.C.
The van was packed when the call came.

"Is this the girl named Ivan?"

How much can you really guess about a stranger's voice on the phone, but I listened to the soft, smiling lilt of hers rise and fall as she explained that she had been at a going away party for me the night before, a surprise going away party that my friends threw for me because I was driving up to the Yukon today to work for six months. Except the surprise part of the plan had worked just a bit too well, because what nobody besides myself knew was that I was teaching twelve inmates at the Burnaby Correctional Centre for Women how to make leather belts all night, and this was the first I had heard about my own party, and it was over. Quite the surprise it was.

"Great party," she explained, and the sound of her laugh made me think of leprechauns. "Anyway, I was going to take the bus up to Whitehorse today, and well, how do you feel about some company? I cooked a whole ton of pasta salad for the bus."

Now, no amount of gas money and pasta salad can pay for four days on the Alaska Highway with someone who is starting to get on your nerves, because after Prince George you really are in the middle of nowhere, but I liked her voice. I said I'd pick her up in an hour at her sister's place on my way out of town.

Of course, driving over, the doubting began. Just me and the open road home—and a perfect stranger. What if she doesn't smoke, or wants to talk about co-dependency or something like that for two thousand miles? She'll be so glad she's not stuck on a Greyhound that she won't actually say anything; she'll just silently roll down her window in a disapproving fashion and say things like, "I should give you my therapist's number. She specializes in addiction issues."

But I picked her up, she bungee-corded her beat-up mountain bike to the roof, loaded in her pasta salad, lit a smoke, and smiled with an elf mouth that matched her leprechaun laugh as she surveyed my van and said:

"So if she breaks down, I guess I'll just double you the rest of the way on my bike."

Three nights later, in a campground somewhere just outside of Fort Nelson, she slipped her tongue into my ear and her right hand into my Levi's and whispered, "I've wanted to do this since we left Kitsilano."

Six months later, I drove back to Vancouver to go to electrical school, and she stayed. She had met a sweet-faced French-Canadian boy who I thought looked like Leif Garrett, and she was, unbeknownst to all of us at the time, pregnant with their first son.

"You gonna write me, Chris?" I asked her as we loaded the last of my stuff back into my van.

"Probably not, but I'll think about you whenever I eat pasta salad, and if that's not love, then I've never been in it."

This is the closest thing to a commitment you will ever get from a leprechaun, and I knew this at the time.

November, 1998 † Whitehorse, Yukon
It is a balmy November day at Chris's cabin, about three below zero and still no snow. The grass is frost-frozen, sparkling under a sun that shines, not cold, but heatlessly, if there is such a word.

Chris wants to get the kids together and dressed and go into town, about a half-hour drive in a four-by-four. You could still make the road right now in a car, but not after a good snowfall.

I haven't seen Francis, her middle son, since he was a

babe in arms. He is now three, and his red brown curls and round face were the first thing I saw at six this morning, when I was still sandpaper-mouthed. He pulled the covers off my face and pronounced in a matter-of-fact falsetto: "I'm not sure who you are, but could you help me out?" His one hand still held the end of the sleeping bag up, and his other hand held a strip of toilet paper, which trailed across the cabin floor and into the cold storage room where I assumed he'd just performed his morning's first production.

Because Francis performs everything. He has just pranced out of his and his brother's bedroom, in a pair of emerald and blue-striped tights, red wool socks, and what looks like part of a sleeve from his dad's old orange sweater stretched up and over his chest, like a tube top.

"Dat dah da dahhh ..." sliding in his socks on the bare floor, his smile flits and then disappears, and he comes to a full halt in front of Chris.

"Francis. Warmer clothes. It's minus three."

His shoulders drop like sandbags, and he stomps, his censored artist head down, back to wardrobe, to change. Thirty seconds later, sliding socks and all, he is back out for act two, but with a purple hippie scarf he is whirling around his neck and twirling ... his red socks making circles and figure eights, he knows no fear of slivers...

"A sweater. For chrissakes, Francis, don't you want to go into town with Ivan?"

Again with the shoulders, and eventually he is forced to compromise his ensemble altogether and submit to a sweater, and a toque as well. I know how he feels—nobody wears a toque and a tube top at the same time, and then to have to cover it all with a sweater?

"What do you think of my three-year-old drag queen, Ivan?" Chris asks me like she is showing me a brand new old car she just bought with her own money. She thinks that he will be my favourite because he is ... well, just like me, and I always thought it would be Emile, because he was the first, and because I was inside of her when he was in her belly and when she came I felt him kick and knew the magic of him then. And then there was Galen, too, and my mom said Chris told her in the truck one day that it was too late for an abortion with him, and that Chris cried when the midwife handed her her third boy, that makes four boys now and her, alone in the cabin, and she knew Galen was going to be the last of it.

But Chris never told me any of this, she just told my mom, and now Galen sits, too, under his crown of cotton ball hair and watches me eat an egg and toast. He is one-and-a-half and drinks cranberry tea from a mug with the rest of us. The kids picked the cranberries themselves.

Galen looks like a little old man shrunk right down, like an owl. There is no baby in his face, and my mom says he will be the most special because Chris almost didn't have him, so he is more of a gift that way. But all Chris tells me is that she has been breast-feeding for five years now, and I couldn't see her in the dark last night when we touched, but her hands felt older.

She smells of wood smoke, and I smell of hair products, and every time I see her the boys are bigger and there is somehow less of her and I meet her sons again, three secrets of her unfolding into their own in a tiny cabin forty miles from anything.

No wonder Chris couldn't wait for me and Francis to meet again. Now that he's walking and talking, and putting on shows. Now that we can relate as equals, he and I. Sure, he's only three, but age has never mattered to a true queen, and it takes one to know one.

Say what you will of nature and nurture and the children of both, scientists and sociologists and endocrinologists and psychologists and psychiatrists and therapists and plastic surgeons can all have their theories, but none of them can explain to me this:

How did Francis get to be Francis in all his Francisness? He doesn't watch TV. He listens to CBC. Francis doesn't know that boys don't wear tube tops. No one has told him this. He just has to wear a sweater too, if it's winter. The magic of this is not lost on me.

He doesn't get it from his father, who doesn't eat anything he doesn't grow, or pick, or preferably shoot, skin, and dress himself with, and his older brother is a five-year-old water-packing, bicepped bushman in his own right, and Galen is only a year and a half.

All four boys seem well aware that Chris is the only female in the house; she owns the only two breasts, the only one without what they have.

Yet Francis, three years old, triumphs like a crocus in a crack in a cliff; how does a lonesome queen even know he exists in a cabin in a frozen field in the Yukon with apparently not another soul around, with an ounce of fashion sense, or even the most minute grasp of the immense and innate drama of it all for miles?

No one but Francis. Until mom drags Uncle Ivan home for a night or two.

This is why I must be there for him, for all those moments, for those drag queen equivalents of baptism, first communion, confirmation, priest, and sainthood, and so on.

The first time he finds the right outfit, the one that really fits, I will hold up the mirror for him and say, "You go, girl." If he wants his ears pierced, he can count on me. The first time he necks with the captain of the basketball team in a closet, I will be his confessor. The first time someone calls him a faggot, and he slowly comes to realize that they don't think a faggot is a good thing to be at all, the first time he feels that fear, I want to be there. I will tell him of the time he was three and first did the red sock circle dance in the orange tube top ensemble. I will tell him then that he was born a special kind of creature, one that God never meant for everyone to understand, but that I understand. I will tell him that I will always love that little flower of him, that perfect unknowing differentness that blossomed and danced in a frozen field in spite of everything.

Because drag queens always dance in spite of everything. It's part of the job description.

How can I look at him and not feel relief? He is living proof that I was just born this way. I don't remember my version of the red sock circle dance, but ten to one someone

125

told me to close my legs because you could see my panties when I danced like that, and how do you spell *unladylike?* But things will be different for Francis, he who will start kindergarten in the year 2000.

Chris and I load the boys into the truck and head into town. I am on a mission: I am taking Francis to meet more of his people.

My friend Cody, the legendary creature with painted nails and black ringlets that reach halfway down his back. It is rumoured that he is a hermaphrodite, that he possesses extra plumbing, perhaps special powers. I have never asked him, because it is none of my business, and Cody has never inquired about the bulge in my own pants. He is a creature of immense grace and beauty, and that is all I need to know.

I take Francis into the cafe where Cody works, to introduce them to each other with all the pomp and circumstance required when in the presence of royalty.

"Cody, I'd like you to meet my godson, Francis. Francis, this is Cody."

But Francis doesn't acknowledge Cody, or his ringlets, or his fingernails at all. Something else more pressing has caught his attention. He reaches his small hand up to caress the fabric of Cody's silver velvet shirt, tight and shimmering over his slender torso. Francis smiles in wonder to himself and his mother places her hand on my shoulder, and laughs like a leprechaun.

"That's my boy," she says, and for a second I am unsure whether she is referring to Francis, Cody, or myself, but it doesn't matter, because we are all where we belong. Home.

I Like to Wear Dresses

I hadn't been to the Yukon for over a year, and had been absent from the fold the last three Christmases. I could hardly wait: I love how rush hour in Whitehorse is seven cars long, and how nobody even thinks about washing their vehicles until the end of May.

I think my body was actually designed to function in minus sixteen degrees Celsius, in the clear, blue cold. I like when the air just starts to sting the backs of your hands, the inside of your nostrils, and the back of your mouth. I love to skate on lakes. It was only December, but I needed a fix to shake the grey edge of Vancouver off my shoulders.

I got a chance to go up for the Longest Night Storytelling Festival and a free plane ticket, so I jumped on it.

I hadn't seen my friend Chris's boys since September 2001, and they were all a foot taller now. During intermission, I snuck the three of them backstage. Galen was five and wide-eyed, standing dwarfed in front of the timpani drums. Emile was nonchalant at eight. "I know that," was how he responded, coolly, to each of my careful explanations of rigging, and scrims, and backlights.

And then there was Francis. Seven now and topped with a crown of red-brown curls, he was most impressed with my solo dressing room and the remnants of the smoke machine's fog backstage from the rock star's set just before the intermission. Francis has recently taken up the ukulele, his mother tells me.

I noticed Francis was wearing just jeans and a t-shirt, even though the show is more than enough reason to dress up. Usually, he never passes up a chance to break out one of his velvet skirts or long-flowing ladies' blouses. My stomach dropped for him. Chris, his mom and one of my fondest loves, told me a few months ago that it has started already. They have started calling him a faggot at school. We knew it was going to happen. I guess we were just hoping it would happen, well, later. He is allowing it to fold up the little flower inside of him. Now he mostly keeps his dresses in the closet and wears them only in the safety and freedom of his own home.

Chris tells me later when the kids are in bed that Francis initially had on his long copper velour lace-up blouse, bell bottoms, and pumps when he heard tonight was going to be Uncle Ivan's big show and they were going to the Arts Centre. When he swooped down the stairs to look for his little mittens on strings, Emile reminded him that Sebastian (from school) was going to be there, too. Francis went back to his room and changed into jeans without a word.

I took him alone (after quite a bit of bickering with his brothers about us needing special time together) to see *The Lord of the Rings: The Two Towers*. I for one am scared shitless of the Dark Riders or Ring Wraiths or whatever, and thought maybe it was too scary for a seven-year-old, but he reminded me politely that I had said he could pick. So he, my big old Cheshire cat-grinning dyke buddy Brenda, and I set off for a little queer quality time together, as per the request of his mother.

Francis wasted little time. He spent three dollars on those plastic eggs with rings and miniature tea cups in them, bought popcorn with his own money, and started asking questions, the first of which were brought on by me going to the bathroom.

Francis had leaned across my empty seat to enquire of Brenda just which washroom I used when out at the movies.

Brenda told Francis that to the best of her knowledge, I utilized the ungendered wheelchair-accessible facilities whenever possible, so as to avoid confusing anyone in the men's room or scaring anyone in the ladies'.

Francis then asked Brenda if she knew for sure if I was a boy or a girl. Francis had asked me this himself on several occasions in the past, and each time I explained myself to him as best I could. I'm not sure if he forgets when I go away, or if he just needs to process it all again as a three-, then five-, and now seven-year-old might. Brenda told Francis that she figured that I was technically a girl, but that I had a whole lot of boy in me as well.

I returned to my seat, and Brenda brought me up to speed on their conversation. Francis's eyes were lit up in recognition and he grabbed my wrist. "I'm just like you, but the reverse." He nodded repeatedly and sat up on his heels in his seat. "I'm a boy, but I have a little girl in me too."

He lowered his voice and looked left, then right, and continued. "I like to wear dresses," he whispered in his most conspiratorial voice.

My heart felt like it was going to climb out of my mouth for the love of him at that moment, and I hugged him over the armrest between us. He was warm and sinewy and smelled just like his brothers, but he isn't. I don't love them any the less for it; it's just that I love him more.

"I know you like to wear dresses, Francis," I said. "I've known you since you were a baby, remember?"

"Since I was inside of my mom? Since Emile was?"

I told him I knew his mom since before she even met his dad, and he shook his head in amazement, like he couldn't fathom a time that long ago.

"Is that why you like to kiss her on the mouth so much all the time?" he asked loudly, in the not-so-innocent way of babes. I shushed him because the movie was starting.

Turns out that *The Two Towers* was too scary for both Francis and me, and at one point he grabbed my hand and bravely whispered, "If this is scaring you too much, I wouldn't mind if you wanted to leave early."

But we stuck it out, and then the three of us drove up Grey Mountain and looked at the tiny, snow-silenced metropolis below us. All the way up the mountain Brenda and I told Francis about our people: those of us who are boys with girls inside, and girls with boys inside, and all of the beautiful in-between and shape shifters that are his ancestors. We told him that since before even his older brother was in his mom's belly, there were people like us.

Brenda told Francis that she was like me too, a girl with a whole lotta man in her, just it was harder to tell with her on account of her gynormous breasts.

"Yes, they are big," he responded almost with reverence at her frame, which for years now has been nicknamed by her friends as Tyrannosaurus Rack. We told Francis that his people have forever been artists and mystics and healers and leaders and librarians.

We talked a lot about bullies and their ways. Francis blew me away, as seven-year-olds are known to do with relatives who don't see them everyday as their brilliance unfolds, by explaining that he reckoned that his bully was mean cuz he'd failed grade two twice already, and his mother drank alcohol when he was in her tummy.

I wondered, as Francis's fairy godfather should, when is too soon to warn my young friend about gay bashers, and how exactly I would go about explaining to a northern boy-girl a thing as incomprehensible as what happened to Aaron Webster, who was found naked in Vancouver's busiest downtown park, beaten to death by a crew of teenagers armed with baseball bats and pool cues. Would I leave out the details, and not mention how the police couldn't find any witnesses brave enough to come forward?

I cried at the sight of his face, so determined, and sure, and self-aware of his difference. So entirely void of shame. I cried with relief in the knowledge that my very existence in his life might make it easier for him to make it all the way through grade three. I cried for the hope he makes me feel, now that I'm not the only cross-dresser born in the Yukon in the family, that I will never be alone again. My own seven-year-old loneliness forged my promise to him to see that things will, indeed, be different for us as a team.

Guess what I got Francis for Christmas? Earrings, both dangly and sparkly ones, and fancy French cologne, the same stuff I wear. It all fits perfectly into the jewellery box he got from his older brother.

A Week Straight

I picked him up at the airport last week. What struck me first was how ugly his hat was. A fleece baseball cap. I blamed his mother, signed the Unaccompanied Minor form they made him wear on a red elastic string around his neck, crammed the offending hat into his overstuffed yellow backpack, and we left. No checked baggage. I love a kid who travels light.

Often when Francis and I hook up, some time has passed since we last saw each other. This time it had only been three months, but when you're seven-and-a-half, three months can hold a decade of things to catch up on. I studied him out of the corner of my eye while driving over the bridge. He was taller, and his legs were beginning to take up more of him than they looked like they should. Stick legs folded into oversized green rubber boots with laces. Very practical footwear. I always appreciated that trait in his mother too. Warm, lined, navy blue rain jacket.

Just a normal little boy, right?

He touches everything, runs his hands over things, opens the glove box, wide-eyed, staring, and pointing at accordion buses. His knees bounce, his head turns, and his fingers tap. Then I see it.

His pinky fingernails are very long. I'm pretty sure that

even Whitehorse Elementary, a notoriously tough place to endure grade two, does not yet have a cocaine problem, even though it is right next to the Quanlin Mall, right in the heart of our throbbing downtown Yukon metropolis. No, I'm pretty sure Francis has long pinky fingernails because somehow, even though there's a guy in grade two who should by age and weight be in grade four who calls him Francis-pees-his-pantses, Francis has managed to keep a hold on something of the smaller boy he once was: the fairy child bedecked in the sunflower-print dress, before public school, divorce, and reality set in, and someone started calling him queer.

He left his dresses at home in a box under his bed, even to come to Vancouver to see me, but he did bring his blue crushed velvet hotpants and velour copper-coloured top. I breathed a sigh of relief that night when he came out of his room dressed for dinner.

I realized at the Value Village the next day how much I had invested in this little boy, how much my heart counted on him making it through school whole. How much I hoped elementary school wouldn't kick the difference right out of him.

We were going to be pirates for the Fool's Parade, and fortunately, I was already quite prepared. A short stop at the home of the girl up the street (not to be confused with the girl next door) produced a virtual pirate's booty of baubles, sashes, and bandanas.

We were searching through the girl's pants in the Village when it happened.

A pair of black, crushed velvet pants with gold lamé parrots embossed around the bell-bottoms. My eyes lit up and I ripped them off the hanger. The perfect pirate pants. Francis ran his hands over them, and I watched his face go from sparkling to something else altogether. A small cloud crossed inside his brown eyes, a picture played behind it in his head, and he shook it out. He made a face and dropped the pants. "A pirate wouldn't wear those," he said with fierce commitment.

"Dude, are you joking? They have parrots on them." I began to argue with this seven-year-old for a minute, and then stopped myself. I was doing what my mother had done. I remembered the summer I turned eleven, and a yellow and grey dress for my Aunt Norah's wedding had me paralyzed in a dressing room. The shopkeeper stood next to my mother pleading, "Come on out, honey, it's okay, I'm sure you look just lovely. It's a beautiful dress, Pat, and one she can wear anywhere."

I had felt panic that day: both at the thought of looking beautiful, and at the very concept of owning a dress that was both "formal enough for a wedding, but not too dressy for school."

I made a promise to myself to always let the boy dress himself how he wanted, even if it was boring and didn't match at all, and bought him the black cargo pants that he thought a pirate should wear.

He did love the tiny little black patent leather dress shoes we found, almost as much as I did, and I took some comfort in that.

We were standing in the line-up the first time it happened. Women talk to you when you have a child with you, and this woman had been watching Francis try on plastic pearls and clip-on earrings as I waited to pay for our booty. She had been checking me out too, and when I caught her, she gave me the old, "Isn't he just a darling" face.

"Now, are we picking out some jewellery for Mom?" she piped up, in that voice used by women who don't have any children anymore.

Francis froze, his shoulders squared, and he returned the pearls to the metal hook they had been hanging on. He looked guilty, maybe, or sad.

"Oh dear, I do hope I haven't said the wrong thing." She reached for my arm and stroked it, and left her hand on the inside of my elbow.

Francis looked like a small child busted doing something he knows everybody thinks is wrong or weird, and my heart broke for him.

The woman thought he was the confused child of a broken home, and thus I was the grieving divorced single father of one, and her heart broke for us.

"Everything is okay with Mom," I said, letting her off the hook. I smiled, which was easy to do when I imagined Chris in her wool army pants and felt jacket, reeking of wood smoke and wearing rubber boots, Francis's string of plastic pearls, and a clip-on hoop earring.

She breathed a sigh of relief. I was just a nice guy taking my boy out shopping for Mom. In the middle of the day. Maybe I was even one of those new-fangled stay-at-home dads.

Me and the kid, we kind of look like each other too.

I began to revel in my new disguise, my new cloak and mirror. A child: proof of my heterosexuality, even if I was a little swishy myself, and apparently it was rubbing off on the kid. At least I was fertile.

I realized this must suck for straighter-looking moms or dads trying to seek a little action, but it was some novelty to me. No one, no matter what gender they mistake me for, ever mistakes me as straight. I might even have a chance to come out of the closet, for the first time ever, I thought with a kind of glee.

I dropped Francis off at the airport yesterday; he was wearing his sensible shoes. Me and four other Spring Break single fathers milled around the security gate, seeing off our respective unaccompanied minors. We called out last-minute reminders to not eat any dairy, and tell your mom to call me, and don't drink any pop even if they give it to you, and tie up your boots. Francis didn't look back as he let the pretty stewardess take his hand.

The guy with the tight pants and John Deere belt buckle's little boy started to bawl, and his dad teared up himself and waved through the glass, yelling, "Daddy loves you," unabashedly. He turned to me and someone's grandparents and said in a choked voice that pulled at the corners of my eyes, "Now, that's harder than a guy would think, huh? Won't see him till September. I'm a merchant marine."

I nodded like I understood, because he thought I did. I felt secretly proud that Francis didn't cry one bit, that in fact my kid was the toughest one of them all.

The Future of Francis

The first time I wrote about my little friend Francis, the little boy who liked to wear dresses, he was three years old. The middle son of one of my most beloved friends, he was the fearless fairy child who provided me with living, pirouetting proof that gender outlaws are just born like that, even in cabins in the bush with no running water or satellite television. He confirmed my theory that some of us come out of the factory without a box or with parts that don't match the directions that tell our parents how we are supposed to be assembled. Watching Francis grow up taught me that what makes him and me different was not bred into us by the absence of a father figure or a domineering mother, or being exposed to too many show tunes or power tools at an impressionable stage in our development. We are not hormonal accidents, evolutional mistakes, or created by a God who would later disown us. Most of us learn at a very early age to keep our secret to ourselves, to try to squeeze into clothes that feel like they belong on someone else's body, and hope that the mean kids at school don't look at us long enough to find something they feel they need to pound out of us. But Francis had a mother who let him wear what he wanted, and Francis had evidence that he was not alone, because Francis had me.

He is eleven now, and I got to hang out with him and his brothers last January, up in Dawson City. He doesn't wear dresses anymore, and I didn't see much of his younger self in the gangly boy body he is growing into. He is a tough guy now, too cool to hug me when his friends are around, full of wisecracks and small-town street smarts. He can ride a unicycle, juggle, and do head spins. He listens to hip-hop and is not afraid to get in a fist fight. He calls other kids faggot, just like his friends do, but only when his mother can't hear him.

I can't help but wonder if the politics of public school have pushed him to conform, or if he has just outgrown his cross-dressing phase and become as butch a son as any father could hope for. I try to imagine what it would be like for him to be the only boy in a dress on a playground full of kids whose parents are trappers and hunters. To be labelled queer in a town of 1,700 people and more than its fair share of souls who survived residential schools, families with four generations of inherited memories of same-sex touches that left scars and shame and secrets. I don't blame him for hiding his difference here, for fighting to fit in.

I walk past his school one day on my way to buy groceries, and watch him kick a frozen soccer ball around in the snow with his buddies. He sees me and stands still for a second, breathing silver clouds of steam into the cold. When he was little, he used to fling himself out his front door when I came to visit and jump on me before I was all the way out of my truck. He would wrap his whole body around my neck and hips and whisper wet secrets and slobber kisses into my ear. Now, he barely returns my wave before he turns and disappears into a sea of snowsuits and scarf-covered faces. I find myself searching the crowd for a boy I barely recognize, a Francis who has outgrown my memory of him. I miss the Francis he used to be, the boy-girl who confessed to me when he was five years old that I was his favourite uncle because we were the same kind of different. Now, I can't tell him apart from all the other boys wearing blue parkas.

I realize later I am doing to Francis exactly what I wish the whole world would stop doing to our children: wanting him to be something he is not, instead of just allowing him to be exactly what he is. I don't want Francis to spend his lunch break being tormented and beaten up. I remember growing my hair in junior high and wanting everyone to like me, and I will never forget the blond boy from school who walked like a girl, and that time in grade eight someone slammed his face in a locker door and gave him a concussion because he wanted to try out for the cheerleading team. By grade ten, he had learned to eat his lunch alone in an empty classroom and wear his gym shorts under his jeans instead of braving the boys' change room, but everybody acted like they were his best friend after he shot himself in the head with his stepfather's hunting rifle during spring break the year we all graduated. They hung his school photo up in the hallway, and all the kids pinned paper flowers and rest in peace notes to the wall around his picture, but nobody wrote that they were sorry for calling him faggot or sticking gum in his hair or making fun of how he threw a ball.

I made a silent promise to Francis the day I left Dawson City to always love what he is right now as much as I loved who he was back then. Whether he grows up to become a textbook heterosexual he-man or one day rediscovers his early love for ladies' garments, I will always be his favourite uncle, no matter what he's wearing.

Four: Kids I Met

Saturdays and Cowboy Hats

Every Saturday morning all summer long, the parking lot across the street from me is transformed. Friday night, it's full of sports cars and sparsely moustached, beer-guzzling boys with cell phones and car stereos that shake the glass in my front windows, but come Saturday morning at eight, it's a farmer's market. There is the fey fella selling homemade dog biscuits, the family-run fireweed honey corporation, the lesbian cheese makers from Saltspring Island, a grumpy potter, and a sunburnt man selling bundles of organic mustard greens and butter lettuce. You can buy cherries and maple syrup, visit the latte wagon, and get gardening advice. You can sign petitions and join a jam-making group that donates to the food bank. There are face painters and banjo players. People wear sandals and the dogs rarely get into fights, because everyone is too busy saying hello and showing off their new bedding plants. Yard sales spring up spontaneously on street corners.

All of this appeals to the increasingly not-so-latent hippie in me. I mean, I still like to wear shoes in the city and I wholeheartedly believe in the frequent washing of one's clothing, but there is still something of the small-towner in me—I like to know my neighbours, I like to meet the guy who picked the cherries I'm about to eat.

I usually throw on a pair of jeans and take the dogs with me. We always complete a loop around the lake before we hit the market, to avoid any unsightly squatting in the middle of the town square.

I saw them getting out of a late model minivan, a young, slender mother and her maybe six-year-old kid. She was in a wind-blown dress that wrapped around her legs, the kid in blue cords with frayed cuffs, a red and yellow striped t-shirt, and now colourless canvas sneakers. The mom had a canvas shopping bag over her shoulder and the kid had a comic book rolled up and pushed into the back pocket of his cords.

"Mom, lookit the little dog, he's sooo wee ..." The little boy bent down to pet my Pomeranian, and his mom stood up straight and slammed the door of the minivan shut.

"Olivia, you have to ask the man if the dog is friendly before you touch it. Maybe it doesn't like little girls."

I looked at the kid again, and she stared back up at me. Her hair was straw yellow, and cut short. She had one hand on her hip, her elbow resting on the comic in her back pocket. The knees of her cords were worn and grass-stained. One shoelace was hanging untied, flattened, and muddied. The only things about her that matched her name were two tiny stud earrings, dark blue and sparkling, out of place with her tomboy face.

I wondered if Olivia got her ears pierced to make Olivia happy, or her mom. Maybe her grandma took her to the salon in a last-ditch feminine attempt to make up for the striped t-shirts and dirty knees.

"She's not a mister, Ma." Olivia spoke matter-of-factly, rolling her eyes back like kids do when their parents say dumb things. "So can I pet your dog, or what?"

I nodded, struck as dumb as her mother. I couldn't make my mouth work, and there were tears in my eyes. I wanted to show Olivia my new fishing rod; I wanted to build her a tree fort with a rope ladder. I wanted to make her a belt with interchangeable brass buckles and teach her how to perfect her wrist shot. I wanted to play street hockey with a tennis ball, and get headaches from eating our Slurpees too fast.

I wanted to pass her a note written in pencil on a piece torn from a brown paper bag that said: YOU ARE NOT THE ONLY ONE. AND ONE DAY EVERYTHING WILL BE FINE, I PROMISE YOU THAT. OH, AND LEARN A TRADE YOU CAN FALL BACK ON.

Olivia's mom stood next to me on the sidewalk. "She really loves little dogs. She's always begging to get one, but we live in a one-bedroom apartment."

Goliath was flat on his back now, all four legs in the air, working the cute angle. Olivia was scratching his belly with both hands.

"Come on, honey, we have to shop. You've got karate at noon. Say goodbye."

Olivia jumped up, wiping her hands on her faded red and yellow shirt. She looked me up and down. Her eyes rested unabashedly on my dusty workboots, then my jeans, my Snap-On Tools belt buckle, the wallet in my back pocket, my black t-shirt, naked earlobes, and freshly shorn hair. She chewed her gum slowly on one side of her mouth and hooked her thumb through an empty belt loop.

"Thanks fer lettin' me pet him. He's real cute, huh? What's his name?"

"Goliath." I could still barely talk, I was still afraid the tears were going to spill over my bottom lids. I wanted her to remember me as being tall and dry-eyed, just in case I was the first one of her people she had met so far.

"It was really nice to meet you, Olivia." I extended my hand, and she shook it, her face deadly serious. Her mother nodded a polite goodbye. Olivia just kept shaking my hand.

"One more thing ..." she said, squinting up at me, the sun bright over my shoulder, "I need to know, where'd ya get that cowboy hat?"

Schooled

Yesterday I spent the day in a high school in Burnaby, telling stories to the grade tens. I was surprised how nervous I was. I tell stories all over the place, often to people who in real life are much more intimidating than a couple hundred fifteen-year-old strangers should be, but right from the time the alarm went off it was there, the big ball of nervous. It hung there in my gut, between my ribs and my belly, all waxy and electric.

The face in the mirror looked pale and rumpled. "That's just perfect," I told my reflection. "A zit. Right in the middle of your chin. On the first day of school."

It's something about the hallways that does it to me, the way sounds are amplified by the polished tiles and painted lockers, all sharp edges and canned echoes. Just the sound of a high school makes me fifteen again.

It didn't help much that all five of us poets and storytellers had to wait in the office for the English teacher to come and escort us to the auditorium. Lined up with our asses slouched in the plastic chairs outside the principal's office, in between the photocopier and the water cooler, the rest of them joked and told anecdotes. I was the quiet one for once, trying to breathe around the inflatable lump in my throat and wondering why my toes were sweating so profusely.

The teacher that had organized the reading was cool; the kind of teacher who would think that poetry in high school was a good thing. Her classroom was the one with the beaded curtain, and the kids who were wrestling or kicking each other in the ass in the hallways didn't straighten up or act like pretend angels when she came around the corner. She explained to us over her shoulder as we walked that the crowd for the lunch-hour show might be a little smaller than they had expected, because today the student council was auctioning off elves in the gymnasium, plus a representative from the community college was answering questions and handing out pamphlets outside the library. We had competition, she told us, but assured us we would have a good house for the afternoon sessions, when attendance was mandatory.

She took us into a place she called the dance room, which meant it looked like a small gym with mirrors lining the walls. She apologized for the fact that we were required to remove our shoes, because they marked up the floor. For some reason this made me uncomfortable. I was about to tell queer stories to a bunch of teenagers, and I wanted my shoes. My sock feet left little sweaty tracks behind if I stood in one place for too long. Two of the other poets were wearing odd socks, and this made me blush. We were here to prove that being a spoken word performer was a viable career option, and I felt that not owning a pair of socks that matched might undermine our position. Then I reminded myself that they had both just come off of a long tour, and I should be glad they were wearing any socks at all. The kids all had to take their shoes off too, which they did in an orderly fashion as they filed into the room. Quite a few of them had on odd socks as well. I changed my position on the matter immediately, thinking maybe it would be something we could bond with them over. Odd socks didn't mean you were poor. Odd socks meant you were a non-conformist.

It turned out that the kids were great. They listened and laughed in all the right places, and asked really smart questions. One kid asked us what the meaning of life was, saying that he had read somewhere that if you asked enough people, one of them might just have an answer. Then he asked me what my favourite Led Zeppelin album was. I told him *Led Zeppelin IV*, and he nodded, like I had passed his invisible test.

Somewhere between classes I relaxed a bit and started to have fun. Sure, there were a couple of kids slouched along one side of the classroom at the back of the room who already could grow sideburns and snickered and rolled their eyes the whole time, but for the most part they were interested, and engaged. I kept telling myself that I wasn't there to change the mind of the beefy guy in the back with the almost full goatee. I was there for the kid I couldn't see yet, the kid who was seeing me for the first time. The kid who walked the edges of the hallways, one hand trailing the lockers and the walls, hoping they won't be waiting for him at the bus stop today. The kid who hides his *Muscle and Fitness* magazines behind a ceiling tile in his closet, when his brothers can read them openly because they are not like him. For the girl who doesn't know yet but her parents do. That was who I was there for.

The cool teacher escorted us through the woodworking shop in between classes to a patchy corner of lawn you couldn't see from any windows in the school, so we could have a smoke. The shop was almost empty, because the bell hadn't rung yet. There was a skinny boy with glasses screwing two bits of wood together with a cordless drill. He nodded at the cool teacher as we shuffled past.

"Hello, Vanessa," the cool teacher nodded back at the kid, and I did a double take. The teacher winked at me, and I smiled. All day, I had been searching for signs that things were different than they were when I was in school, that things were getting easier for queer kids, that we really had come a long way, baby. I had overlooked the most obvious sign. Of course things were changing. I was here, wasn't I?

Teach the Children Well

Every time I do a storytelling gig at a public school, I swear to myself that I will never do it again. I promise myself that this is the last time, that the next time they ask me I will remember that I have decided to avoid attempting to entertain large groups of teenagers for health reasons, that breathing gymnasium air makes me dangerously dehydrated, that hallways lined with lockers can cause painful grade eight flashbacks. High schools remind me of high school, I can't help it. I graduated twenty years ago, but all it takes is the sound of the first period buzzer going off or the smell of floor wax and it is 1985 all over again, when I am skinny and self-conscious. I hate my legs, my flat hair, my flat chest, my chipped front tooth. I am scared of change rooms and crowded cafeterias. I am scared of myself, of the secret heart inside me that doesn't beat like it is supposed to and makes me different. I don't know I'm queer yet, but I know what happens to kids who don't fit in.

Every time I walk through the front doors of another high school, I remember what it was like to hide, to pretend, to practice not being different. I watch the kids, noticing the ones who avoid my eyes instead of staring. I am not here to change the minds of the many. I am here for the kids who think they are alone. The skinny boy with the long eyelashes who knew he was a fag even before they started calling him one in gym class. The Catholic girl who confesses only to her journal and prays that God will make it go away. The oldest daughter of a former beauty queen whose mother makes her see a shrink once a week ever since she got busted French kissing a girl named Marie on the couch in the rec room when they were supposed to be working on a three-dimensional model of a molecule. These are the kids I want to be seen by, the kids I want to stand in front of, unashamed and unafraid. I don't say I'm queer, because I don't need to. I wear cowboy shirts and big black boots and tell stories. I tell them that my writing pays all my bills, that I love my job, that they can be artists too, not just lawyers and dentists and assistant managers.

A couple of months ago, I got an email from an English teacher asking me to come and perform in a high school in Surrey, the conservative town situated southeast of Vancouver. Surrey, with a school board prone to banning books with titles like *Heather Has Two Mommies*. Did I want to risk a gig in Surrey? Absolutely not. I was halfway through writing a polite letter saying that I was busy that day, when I stopped to consider what school must be like there for young homos. How could I turn my back on the queer kids who needed me most? How often was a gay storyteller even allowed inside a high school in Surrey? I said yes, and immediately started to stress out about it. I arranged to bring my friend the punk-rock cello player with me, for moral and musical support.

A couple of weeks before the gig, I got another email from the English teacher. He explained that one of the other teachers had done some research on me and had raised concerns about "inappropriate sexual content" in my work, and would I mind sending copies of all the stories I was planning to read so that the staff could make sure I wouldn't say anything that might offend anyone? There would be a couple of Mormon kids in the audience, he added, and the school wanted to avoid any trouble.

I took a deep breath, smoked two cigarettes, and called him on the phone. I liked him, and I knew he meant well. I told him that the reason I do gigs in high schools is to show the kids that being an artist is a viable career option, to inspire them to believe that writing or painting or playing an instrument is just as important as algebra or volleyball. I told him that I would never do or say anything that would jeopardize the chance to bring other artists into his school, and that I was there to encourage creativity, not homosexuality. I told him that I wouldn't say anything too gay, but that I looked queer and if looking queer was also against school rules then I could recommend another talented storyteller who also might offend the Mormon kids because he is from the Dogrib First Nation and believes in magic and different gods, but at least he was heterosexual.

So the cello player and I did two one-hour sets in a Surrey school last week. I told wholesome stories, and she swore once in one of her songs, but none of the teachers batted an eye, they were so relieved that we didn't bring up how obviously queer we both were. The principal gave us

154

each a mug and a matching pen, and a thank-you card with a cheque inside.

That night we both received MySpace messages from the girl with the purple brush-cut who sat in the front row during the afternoon set. She was smiling in her picture, her cheek pressed up against her girlfriend, who had orange hair and a nose ring. She was just writing to tell us how much she loved our show; that it was the best thing her school had ever seen. I clicked on her profile. It said she was sixteen, a lesbian, and an aspiring writer.

This Summer, at Gay Camp

He shone like a brand new dime, that first time. "I want you to meet my son," she had told me. "I want him to meet more gay people. School has been hard on him these last couple of years."

I was in Fort Smith, Northwest Territories, on tour with a mismatched set of other storytellers. It was the first week of June, and the roof of the earth was gearing up for summer solstice. The midnight sun stretched the light so far and long that dusk was bent over backward enough to bump into the next day. The sun cooked the dirt into dust that got into everything, grinding between back teeth and turning my new black boots grey. We were a seven-hour drive by mostly gravel road to Yellowknife. A hell of a place to try to hide yourself. A hell of a place to have to repeat grade ten.

His mother was a solid, smiling Métis woman with a laugh you could hear from the other side of the lake. Her son stepped out of the car and onto the weary pavement of the parking lot outside of the only motel in town, which boasted a restaurant that served both Chinese and Italian cuisine, and I use the term loosely.

He was wearing brand new sneakers, so white they caught the sunlight and bounced it right back, bleaching the backs of my eyelids when I closed them. His tracksuit was also white, both pieces, and so was the singlet he had on underneath. All of his clothes were crisp and pristine, with a fresh-out-of-the-wrapper look that stood out stark and sudden against the frayed and aging backdrop of this little northern town.

He was sapling thin, with cover girl cheekbones and feather duster lashes. Easily one of the prettiest boys I had ever seen, all long fingers and fey hips and wrists. I could imagine him standing in a line-up on Davie Street in Vancouver, waiting to get into a club that would be pounding a dull bassline from inside, surrounded by his twinkie buddies in designer jeans and two-hundred-dollar t-shirts. That such a creature still breathed in a high school in Fort Smith, Northwest Territories, seemed somehow unfathomable to me.

A mud-coloured pick-up pulled up beside us, its tires popping bits of loose gravel sideways. Our hiking guide jumped down from the driver's seat, wearing sturdy boots and a grey beard. He led us on a meandering route past the old graveyard and down a well-worn path through the pines, wide shards of sunlight showing the dust and dandelion seeds floating in the air that smelled so much like home to me. I kept stealing looks at my friend's fairy boy son, him in his immaculate threads and me in my now dirty new Fleuvog boots and vintage leather coat. I loved him at first sight, flying his flaming flag so fiercely, here, so far from a pride parade or leather bar or Mac counter. All of fifteen years old and fearless already.

Later, I pulled his mother aside and told her about a

camp in Edmonton for gay youth where I was going to be artist-in-residence in a couple of weeks. It was probably too late for this year, I told her, but what the hell, send in an application, because you never know.

The last week in July, he sashayed through the door of the education centre in Edmonton. Sixty-five queer youth for four days. I wondered if he had ever been around more than one or two queer people at the same time before. I wondered if he felt as overwhelmed as I did. A place where faggot wasn't a bad word anymore. A place where he could be one of many. A place where he could just be.

I got to work, teaching creative writing classes every morning and cajoling my group of youth to choreograph an a cappella synchronized dance number to "I Will Survive." He was in my group, and I spent the better part of four days trying not to hug him too much in front of everybody else.

On Saturday night there was a talent show. One of the local kids organized a fashion show, and he modeled a gold lamé gown complete with fake breasts and walked the runway in heels like he was born in them. I felt like the homosexual version of a hockey dad whose son has just scored in overtime.

I watched him stand taller and smile bigger and swish wider every day. And then, of course, the inevitable came around.

Sunday night. There was a lot of crying, the kind of tears that could only be conjured up by a bunch of queer kids about to return to High River and Moose Jaw and some little town just north of Edmonton. Alone.

I couldn't even look him in the eyes the last time I hugged him. I couldn't tell him what I was thinking. I hoped that the new pride he held in his shoulders wasn't going to be pounded out of him in gym class, or while he tried to learn trigonometry. I felt sad, but mostly I felt rage. Rage that we are beginning the second decade of the twenty-first century in what is supposed to be one of the most liberal and progressive countries in the world and still we haven't made our schools safe for kids like him. That something as vital to his future as his education happens in a culture of fear and under the threat of violence.

I reminded myself to be thankful that at least he has what a lot of queer kids don't have: an amazing family behind him. I got an e-mail from his mom yesterday. She thanked me for getting him into camp, saying that he really needed this support, and that he seemed so much more confident and wiser since he came home.

The four days of relative safety and acceptance from his peers really did him some good. Now we just have to get to work on the other 361 days of the year. He still has grade ten to get through. Again.

Straight Teens Talk Queer

Recently I had the pleasure of being a teen mentor for a group of nine youths at the Vancouver Public Library's annual book camp. My kids were almost frighteningly smart, and savvy, and hilarious, and of course, well-read.

I decided I was going to put all that intelligence and potential and Internet virtuosity to work and get them to write my column for me this month. We set out to write a piece about homophobia from the point of view of a group of predominantly heterosexual youths. As they were a rather studious lot, we started off by not only defining homophobia for the reader, but by including a historical overview of how definitions of the word homophobia might have changed over the years. Turns out that in 1958, there was no such word as homophobia listed in *The Comprehensive Word Guide*; all the kids could find was a definition of homosexuality listed under "certain specific sexual aberrations, perversions, abnormal practices, etc." alongside thirty-nine other practices which included bestiality, auto-fellatio, cunnilingus, and coprolagnia, which none of us had ever heard of, but we looked it up. Look it up. I dare you.

We all found it notable that a mere fifty years later, *Webster's* defined homophobia as "the fear of or contempt for lesbians and gay men, or behavior based on such a feeling."

We then came up with a list of questions, and everybody took them home for homework. This was followed the next day by a rather raucous and ridiculously funny discussion resulting in all of us being resoundingly shushed twice, because we were, after all, in a library. Here is a list of the questions and a sampling of their answers.

Do you think that homophobia still exists in our society?

Sarah, age sixteen: It may not be as harsh as it was in the past, but it is still there. People in the gay community are not always beaten for being who they are but they are definitely not always welcomed by all the people around them.

Wednesday, seventeen: Being a high school student myself I can safely say yes, it does. I do believe that acceptance is a lot more common than it was twenty, or even ten years ago. Things are definitely looking up. I see straight boys with their arms around each other as a sign of affection, I see boys wearing pink and not getting called the F word. I see girls holding hands and no one is writing accusatory labels on their lockers.

Why do you think homophobia still exists?

Megan, sixteen: I blame religion, or, more accurately, religious fanatics.

Sarah: Not all cultures suppressed it for thousands of years. In Greece they used to wrestle naked. That's how the Olympics got started.

Olivia, fifteen: People prefer the ordinary.

Annalise, fifteen: Some people are closed-minded and not accepting of what is different and strange to them.

Kylee, seventeen: It's all Adam and Eve stuff. People are afraid that if they allow it to happen God will be angry and bring damnation or something down upon them.

Wednesday: I'm not sure that there is only one thing or person to blame, unless you can blame the entire human race and call it a night. But that won't bring back the numerous suicides, and it won't make things any better.

Julian, fifteen: Some bigotry is rooted deeper than just in ignorance, but hopefully those people will eventually succumb to the inevitable and keep their mouths shut.

Do you want to end homophobia, if indeed you feel it still exists? Why?

Sarah: Of course I want it to end.

Neil, seventeen: Why should straight people care? Why do white people care that we are mean to black people? It's a moral issue and we have accepted that it is not okay to discriminate ... period.

Does homophobia impact your life in any way, or anyone who you know or care about?

Sarah: One of my best friends felt so afraid of what would happen to him in my town that he felt the need to move. I haven't seen him in over two years.

Lisa, sixteen: I've grown up in a family that says they find nothing wrong with it, but have some serious issues, and I feel embarrassed. I meet these truly interesting and inspiring people, and it hurts to learn that they have been treated wrongly, especially when I hear the slander coming from the mouths of people I respect and trust. What if, somewhere down the line, I realize that I'm not heterosexual? I won't have a problem with it, but what of my friends and family? Will they be supportive or turn their backs? *Give an example of ways we could change things.*

Sarah: My school tries to stop people from using the term gay in a derogatory fashion by making the student who uses the word write a 5,000-word essay on why the use of that word could be offensive. But I don't think this works because it is hardly ever done or checked up on.

Julian: The fact that Gay/Straight Alliance groups can exist is a sign of the times. Fifty years ago, such groups would have been counterproductive: instead of a safe place, these groups would have been bull's-eyes.

Annalise: Set an example of not being homophobic, and not making homophobic remarks, and hope that others take on that acceptance too.

Megan: My school has a program on sexual orientation; they mix it in with sex ed and suicide awareness. The leaders asked us what we would do if we found out one of our friends were gay. If you were okay, you went to one side of the room; if you weren't, you went to the other side of the room. Only one person stayed on the not okay side.

So. There you have it. I think there is only one right thing to do with our society. We have to turn it over to these people. Which is great, because eventually this is going to happen anyway, whether the rest of us are ready for it or not.

My Name is Sam

I was smoking a cigarette with the performance poet outside the theatre. She smokes like a movie star, making sweeping semicircles with her forearms and revealing glamorous cheekbones with every inhale. When she exhales, a perfectly lipsticked stream of silver escapes her mouth between bits of story. I could watch her smoke until the sun showed up. I'm a Player's Light regular peasant; she's a Benson and Hedges Ultra Light King Size Menthol diva.

We were interrupted by a squeal that belonged to a permed and tinted blonde in a beige pantsuit and dyed-to-match pumps. She sniffed her way through our smoking circle to kiss the poet on both cheeks and hug her without really touching.

"Oh my God," the blonde exclaimed, "I thought that was you. You look fabulous. Haven't changed a bit. It's been a long time. When did we graduate? Nineteen seventy ..."

The poet blanched, and interrupted her. "Ivan, this is ..."

"Diane. I'm Diane. We went to high school together. Oh, I could tell you some stories."

The poet cleared her throat and took a long drag from her cigarette. "Well, actually, Diane, you graduated a few years ahead of me."

Diane looked confused. I smiled. The performance poet has been lying to me about her age for several years now, and for me to do the math at this juncture would be ungentlemanly. To know her age in people years would be tantamount to seeing the bride in her dress before the ceremony. She is beautiful years old according to the diva calendar, and that is all I've ever needed to know.

Diane changes the subject. "Well, I married Richard of course, we have one son, twenty-three, and one daughter, twenty-one. They're both at the University of Alberta, doing well, and I'm directing *Fiddler on the Roof* this summer, in the park right across the street. You should come by one night. We're having a gas. The kids are just great. And you, are you still writing poetry?"

"Always." The poet exhales, blinking.

"How interesting. We should do lunch one day, I'd love to hear all about it. Call me. I should be off, though, to round up the kids. It was nice to meet you."

And she was gone, leaving only a hint of Oscar de la Renta in the air.

"She's much older than me," the poet whispered over the sound of Diane's pumps retreating.

"Quite obviously so." I grind my cigarette under the heel of my Daytons. "Let's head in. I'm on in half an hour."

Right at the end of my set, I heard a small kerfuffle in the balcony. It was over quickly, and I thought no more of it.

Post-show, we resumed our spot in the smokers circle, several hours and two beers later. There were five or six of us now, talking poetry, gossip, and business.

A teenage boy paced around our circle a couple of times, took one huge breath, strode up and stood beside me. He seemed nervous, his hands stuffed deep into the pockets of his too-big-for-him black blazer. He waited for a pause in the conversation, and then placed a long-fingered hand on my forearm.

"Sorry to interrupt you," he stammered. "But I have to thank you for your stories tonight. You just changed my life. My life is changed now. I really needed to hear what you just said. I'm a huge fan of spoken word and poetry."

I tuned out everyone else except the boy. This was one of those moments, I could tell, one of those moments you conjure up when you're trying to sleep on the cat pee-scented couch in a chilly basement room on tour somewhere in Manitoba, to remind yourself why you choose to do this for a living. I extended my hand to him.

"My name is Sam. I've been reading Ferlinghetti and Rilke for years, and I'm a huge fan of Sheri-D ..." He shook my hand with baby-soft palms. His bangs hung over his caterpillar lashes and brown eyes. He had a peace sign and a Sex Pistols button on his lapel. The knees of his jeans were peeled back to reveal doorknob kneecaps. His dress shoes were spit-shined. I loved him.

"This is Sheri-D right here, I'll introduce you ... she doesn't bite, well, not strangers, anyway."

I tapped on the performance poet's elbow. "Sheri-D, I'd like you to meet Sam. He loves poetry."

Sam swallowed, overwhelmed. "Wow, pleased to meet you, all of you, the show was, well, it blew my mind, and

I'd do it all over again, it was worth it all, even though I got into trouble."

Sheri-D furrowed her brow and looked sideways at Sam. "You got into trouble for coming to a poetry reading?"

"Well, I skipped out of our meeting after my show. I'm in the play across the street, in the park. I'm the boyfriend of the milkman's daughter."

Suddenly Diane and her pumps and perm were upon us again. "There you are Sam, good, I wanted to talk to you. I want you to know, I'm not angry with you, just disappointed. You can't take off like that without telling anyone where you are going. We were all concerned for your safety. This is downtown Calgary, and I am responsible for all of you. We had to call the police, and security."

The whole picture became apparent to both Sheri-D and I at the same time, and we simultaneously clutched our aching chests with our right hands. Sheri-D spoke first.

"Sam is in trouble for skipping his notes to come and see Ivan tell stories?"

I thought about all the things I ever got busted for when I was fifteen. Poetry readings were not among them. My heart opened and swallowed Sam up.

Diane nodded. "We had to have security remove him from the theatre. They serve alcohol in there. We were looking all over for him. He's been suspended from the play for two nights."

"I'll leave you two tickets at the door for tomorrow night then." Sheri-D smiled at Sam. Diane fixed an acid stare on Sheri-D. "Well, he might as well, since he's not working,"

Sheri-D shrugged.

I nodded. The boy needed poetry, that much was obvious.

"It is time to get you home, Sam." Diane grabbed the sleeve of his jacket and steered him towards her mini-van.

Sam called back over his shoulder to us as he was led away by one arm. "I'd do it all again. I loved it. They call me Art Fag at school." The sliding door shut, and he was gone.

"What a bitch," Sheri-D breathed sideways at me. "No wonder she looks so much older than I do."

"Decades," I agreed, and lit her next cigarette for her.

Nobody Ever

It was raining the day I met her. The kind of rain that hits the pavement and puddles so hard it bounces back at the sky, backward and defiant. It was the kind of evening best spent inside, but there she was, standing soggy on the sidewalk, waiting to talk to me.

As soon as I emerged from the back door of the theatre, she speed-walked in a straight line towards me. Her name was Ruby, she told me, and she was from a small town, about three hours' drive from here. She was almost twelve years old and she wanted to be a firefighter when she grew up, or maybe a marine biologist. Her mom had driven her here, so she could see me perform at the Capitol Theater. It had said on my website that I was going to be reading in Olympia, Washington, and since it was a Saturday and there was no school she had made her mom drive her all this way for my show, but then it turned out that since they were selling alcohol in the theatre she wasn't allowed inside, not until she turned twenty-one, anyways, which was like, ten years away, practically.

She took a deep breath, and continued. She had seen me at the folk festival in Vancouver last summer, and I had read a story about a tomboy I had met at the farmers' market, did I remember the one?

I nodded, yes, I did.

She shifted her weight from one sneakered foot to the other and back again, like she needed to pee, and flipped her head back to shake her shaggy bangs out of her eyes. She blurted out her words like machine gun bullets, like she had been rehearsing them for a while, her mouth pursed in a determined little raisin.

When she first heard that story, well, she was just amazed, she told me. She had begged her mom to buy her all of my books right there on the spot, but her mom only had enough money for one. She had to wait until it was her birthday, which was October by the way, until she could get my next book, and then she got one more from her aunt at Christmas, but when was I going to put out a new one? She liked them all, nearly the same amount, except for *Loose End*, which of course was her favourite because it had the story "Saturdays and Cowboy Hats" in it, which was the very first story of mine she ever found out about, when she heard me at the park in Vancouver last summer but she had already told me that part.

By this time I was ready to scoop Ruby up in my arms and hug her, but I didn't, because her mom was waiting in the car parked two feet away from where we were standing and I thought it might seem weird.

Ruby stepped sideways, farther under the awning over the door of the theatre. She pulled a love-worn copy of my book out from her rain jacket, and held it out to me.

"Could you sign it for me? To Ruby, Love from Ivan? You could say, To my biggest fan, Ruby, too, if you felt like it. Whatever you want."

I wrote "To Ruby, my biggest fan, Love from your biggest fan, Ivan," and passed it back to her. She tucked it under her armpit for safekeeping. Her fingernails were bitten right down to the quick, just like mine used to be.

"Thanks. I really love your books a lot. Especially the one about the tomboy, cuz, well, the little girl in that story, she reminds me of me." She paused for a second, met my eyes with hers, and held them there. "And nobody ever reminds me of me."

I stepped back out into the rain, hoping that it would look like raindrops sliding down my cheeks, not big hot tears. I pulled one of my CDs out of my bag and passed it to her.

"Here you go, this should hold you until the new book is out."

The last time I saw Ruby, she was waving backwards at me from the passenger seat of a beat-up station wagon. Her mom honked the horn twice goodbye as they turned and disappeared around the corner.

A while ago I was reading at a fundraising dinner in Ottawa, and I met a woman named Hilary. Hilary was in her fifties I would say, wearing black boots and old jeans. She used to own her own house painting company, but she was retired now. I liked how she shook my hand too hard, how the skin of her palms was still callused, how she spooned too much sugar into her coffee. I liked how she ate her salad with her dinner fork and didn't care. Her hair was just getting long enough to brush the collar of her dress shirt and hang over the tops of her ears. This probably bothered her, and she probably had an appointment to get it cut early next week, before it got totally out of hand.

After the gig was over, she helped me pack the rest of my books out to my truck. We talked about everything and nothing: what it used to be like working on a job site twenty years ago, how it is better now but not by much, what a difference a good pair of snow tires can make, how the old back just ain't what it used to be, stuff like that.

The snow was falling in fat lazy flakes. The parking lot was empty, except for two trucks, one hers, the other mine. Finally, she shook my hand hard one last time and then pulled me into a hug.

"Make sure you keep in touch," she told me. "It was great to meet you. You remind me of me when I was a kid."

As Good As We Can Make It

I have been a road dog lately. Festivals, theatres, conferences, planes, boats, rental cars, road and road and then some more road. And schools. I have been doing a lot of high school gigs too. Sometimes I wonder if maybe I get the opportunity to see the insides and the guts of more high schools, and shake hands with more students, and stumble through more uncomfortable introductions to more principals, and cover more territory, span more provinces and borders and districts and countries, even, than almost anyone working in our education system today. Sure, it's quick and I am there and then gone in a little under two hours, mostly, but still. You get a sense of a place, a taste of it, anyway, and more and more I am sampling the smorgasbord of our school system, and where it best serves our students, and where it is still falling short.

I do a one-hour show, designed to fit in between bells, forty-five minutes or so of storytelling, followed by a ten- to fifteen-minute question-and-answer and hopefully discussion period.

I don't say the word queer or gay or lesbian during this show, nor do I talk about sexuality at all. I just tell stories. Stories about me, my little sister, and my two little cousins, Dan and Christopher. Christopher was an awkward, clumsy kid who was mercilessly teased and picked on all throughout school, right from the beginning. I tell stories about the four of us, stuff we used to do when we were young, stupid broke-ass bored small-town kid stuff. I tell the story about how Christopher had gigantic feet for his age, size thirteen by the time he was eight years old, and about how we all got second-hand roller skates this one summer, all of us except Christopher, who could not cram his gigantic feet into the cool roller skates, so we had to buy him those crappy old-fashioned kind that you had to buckle up over your own shoes, and anyway long story short, he wipes out and craps his pants. Of course, all of us love a good poop-your-pants story, right? It's a classic, I believe, the great leveler. We all pooped our pants when we were babies, and then accidentally here and there throughout our lives, and of course every single one of us is gonna shit ourselves again at some point on our way out of this world, unless it happens very quickly and we never see it coming, so in this way pooping yourself is one of those things that makes us all human, together.

Needless to say this story goes over well with the kids, and I achieve my primary objective, which is to get them all to identify somehow with my clumsy and unlucky little cousin, to invest in him somehow, to care about him, to sympathize. Hopefully we laugh together. Then I sit back and wait for the question, which almost always comes. Almost every show some kid puts up their hand and asks me where is Christopher now?

Where is Christopher now? I tell them that I know what

they want me to tell them. I tell them I really wish I could tell them what I know they want to hear. I say how much I wish I could tell them that my little clumsy cousin Christopher grew into his gigantic feet and eventually became a tall and handsome man, who would one day marry a tall handsome woman and they had two tall handsome children and now he lives happily in a suburb somewhere and works at his successful and fulfilling job in the IT industry, and that they have a little brown dog and a white picket fence, but I can't. I can't tell them that because Christopher died on Christmas Eve in his twenty-first year of a self-inflicted gunshot wound to the head, and that is why I come into high schools. That I want them all to know that someone cares about them, and that they have a right to access their public education without threat of physical, emotional, or spiritual violence. Then we talk about bullying, and what we can all do to work towards building a safe and respectful learning environment for each and every one of them.

Recently I was in St. John's, Newfoundland for a storytelling festival. This festival has historically asked all of their performers do a few school gigs while they are in town. But a couple of weeks ago the festival director called me up to inform me that six St. John's schools had turned down my show, even though the festival was going to pay my fee and it would have cost these schools nothing. She was a little embarrassed about the whole situation. Said this had never happened before. Said the principals were concerned that I might upset certain parents, that perhaps I was ... not appropriate, somehow, for a high school environment. So. I ended up doing only two school shows in St. John's, the only two schools that would have me, which were the Catholic school, ironically, and an alternative school for kids who had dropped out of the public school system altogether, many of whom had been bullied right out of an education, and/or battled learning disabilities or other challenges. Both shows were amazing, full of good discussions and intelligent questions. It was a great way to spend a Thursday.

But that very same Thursday night in St. John's, the unthinkable happened. One of the students from a school that had turned down my anti-bullying show took his own life. I don't know him, never had the chance to meet him. I don't know if he was gay, or even if he was bullied, and now I will never know. But obviously something was going on for him. There is no way to know if a one-hour storytelling show and discussion might have changed this terrible outcome for this boy, and his family, and his friends and fellow students, who will all carry his death now for the rest of their lives. How do I know this? Because I carry my cousin's, it is right here with me now. I don't know that my show would have changed anything. I don't know that. But what really haunts me is that I don't know that it wouldn't have helped him, either. I send my compassion and love out to his family and classmates. What will it take for school administrations to realize that providing a safe school environment for all is more important than catering to the bigotries of the few?

I want to share part of an article that my friend Matt Pearson, an Ottawa writer and journalist, published, called "The Arithmetic of Shame." Matthew writes:

"You may have read or seen on the news recently that a teenage boy in Ottawa took his own life after struggling for some time with depression and the challenges of being the only openly gay student at his suburban high school. I covered the tragic story as a reporter for a daily newspaper and have remained troubled by it for days afterward.

"I did not know this child. But what I do know, at least in part, was the depth of despair he too often felt. It mirrored what I felt more than 15 years ago as a confused and pimply teen growing up in Woodstock, Ontario.

"At my Catholic elementary school, I was called names on the playground years before understanding the full and hurtful meaning of them. I was made to feel different—and not in a good way—because I preferred drama, hung out mostly with girls and didn't like rough-and-tumble competitive sports. I soon became isolated. I developed a deep sense that even if I didn't quite know what those words meant, it must have been something pretty awful, judging by the way some boys I had known for years spit them at me.

"I started bringing candy and bubble gum to school to give out freely on the playground at recess. Later, I became one of those chauffeur teens, always glad to give someone a ride somewhere, even if it was way out of my way.

"This is the arithmetic of shame. The subconscious calculations I made in hopes people could find in me enough good things to compensate for the one unspeakably ugly part.

"I switched to the public school system for high school and hoped my troubles were behind me, as most of my classmates continued on to the Catholic high school.

"But it only got worse. I know now, years later, that high school sucks for just about everyone, but back then, I thought it was my own private hell. The verbal harassment was almost unbearable and came from people—often boys, but sometimes girls, too—who I'd never even seen before. How could they know something about me that I was only beginning to understand?

"I was never physically beaten up, which is a good thing because far too many young people are victims of assault. But while it may seem masochistic, I often wished I was because then perhaps my teachers and fellow students would see for themselves the black eyes and bruises of hate.

"There were hallways, nooks and crannies in that school where I never dared to go, especially on my own. And this was a school where my father—a kind man who has loved and supported me unconditionally since the day I came out a dozen years ago—was principal. I know it still pains him that he could not protect me."

Last year I had a gig in a Vancouver area high school. It was for the Dare to Stand Out conference, a gathering of LGBTQ students and their queer or ally teachers.

Even though I was in a high school for an explicitly homo positive event, I still had the familiar heart-pound-mouth-dry-watch-my-back feeling descend upon me as I entered through the double glass doors and past the school office, and followed the rainbow signs that led me into the gymnasium.

I was an adult, and I was about to speak to a bunch of queer kids and teachers. I had officially been out of school for longer than I was ever in school, but still, my body's memory took over, and took me back. Back to my own sixteen-year-old self. How do I know that I still need to work to make schools safer for all kids? Because I am still afraid of entering a high school, to this day, even now, even for something like this.

My nerves quickly disappeared when I walked into the gym and saw the sixteen-year-old pretty boy with the Mohawk and the eyeliner who was setting up the mikes. Not to mention the awesome kick-ass young woman behind the soundboard, whose nametag read Darth Vader, and her sidekick, dubbed Stormtrooper, of course.

Our next generation. I love them all, just on principle, and feel fiercely, almost irrationally protective of them. I want everything to be so much different for them than it was for us. I want them to be able to be unapologetically out and safe in their schools, and I want them to feel nothing but memories of joy and triumph should they ever return to a high school for any reason twenty some years from now. I know, what a dreamer, right? But why not? Why not imagine building a safe, respectful environment for all kids to be educated in right now? Why expect anything less, and why settle? Because we had to? That is simply not good enough. The fact that so many of us, queer or fat or nerdy or smart or slow or brown or from somewhere that is not here, still can't imagine school without the accompanying torment or hassle or trauma is a sign to me of just how much work we still need to do in our schools for all kids, not just the queer ones.

This is the gist of what I said to all those young and beautifully out-already faces that day:

1. Always remember that working to make your school safer for queer students, or bisexual students, or gender non-conforming students is not a selfish act. Creating a safe school for yourself will only lead to a safer school for everyone, and everyone deserves a safe place to learn in. Not feeling safe at school can seriously affect your ability to access your own education, which can impact your life for the rest of your life. When you work to make your school better for you, you are doing your school, and everyone in it, and everyone who will ever be in it in the future, a gigantic favour. Never forget that.

2. You deserve so much more than to just be tolerated. You deserve to be loved for exactly who and what you are right now. This is, of course, a double-edged sword. This also means you must return the favour. Learn about racism and sexism and ableism too. You unfortunately are probably already well aware of how much homophobia can hurt, inside and out. Learning more about how different kinds of oppression work and where they intersect will help you build better bridges with others and create a safe and respectful school culture for everyone. Bullies are almost always outnumbered by the bullied. We just need to organize.

3. Remember that not everyone is able to come out to everyone all of the time. Some of us cannot come out to our parents yet, or our employers, or our teammates, or even our friends. It is okay to know who you are and keep it

private if your own safety requires it. This does not mean you are any less queer or radical or cool than the guy with the purple hair and the rainbow stockings. It just means that he has different circumstances than you do.

4. It does get better. Especially when you make it better. There are lots of us out there who care a whole lot about you, whether it feels like it sometimes or not. I am one of them, and I will never stop coming into high schools to meet kids just like you, until I stop feeling scared every freaking time I walk through those front doors, I will keep working to make all schools safer for all of us. I promise you that.

And in the meantime, when I get home I will watch It Gets Better videos, not because they are any kind of a real solution, but because they make me, a comfortably out-for-almost-twenty-five-years adult, feel a whole lot better, so I can get up the next day and get to work, actually making it better.

I really love the It Gets Better series—I know we need these stories, that they can be accessed from any public computer, and that kids need them. But now I want to hear from some from straight kids, adults, teachers—vowing to grow up, step up and *make* it better. I want to hear stories about straight kids who have moved from fear to humanity and stood up to become allies, I want adult former haters to tell conversion stories.

I want teachers who are finally so ashamed of pretending this isn't a literacy issue to challenge other teachers by making their classrooms a place where ignorance and fear are met with information and compassion.

I am sick of moving people to tears with stories of casualties from the warfare we let our children wage on each other. I am sick of young dead boys becoming icons of public compassion, and inspiring Rick Mercer rants we can share with each other on Facebook, while at the same time we continue to allow our principals and school administrators to cater to the conservative and religious right and pretend that our kids don't all pay the price for their apathy and cowardice.

Bullies grow up—their behaviour gets modified and sometimes their language gets slicked over with education—and they become the political, financial, and social arbiters of life as we know it. I bet you any money that Prime Minister Stephen Harper was a bully in school, and don't we all wish now that someone had nipped him in the bud before it was too late for Canada.

It is time for us to write ourselves some new stories, people. So, let me tell you one.

Last year I was invited to a high school on the west side of Vancouver. The rich part. It was an arts-enhanced school, and I had been asked to come in specifically because one of the students there was transitioning, in grade nine, and they were throwing him a birthday party. Not because it was his actual birthday, but because he was being reborn. The school threw him a party, and bought him a cake. They informed the entire student body of his new name, his pronoun preference, and that he would now be using the boy's washroom. Amazing, right? I cried throughout most of that day. Hope, relief, and redemption, palpable, caught in my throat, pounding in my heart. Just because I got to see one good story, for a change. But what a change, indeed.

What did the school spend to make that kid's life so much better? The cost of one birthday cake, that is what they spent. And what did they save? Maybe his life, or maybe the lives of countless other kids who took heart and hope that maybe school and life doesn't suck as hard as it did yesterday. Maybe school and life were worth sticking around for after all.

Ask me now, how important it is for queer teachers and school staff to come out of the closet? How important it is for queer athletes and rock stars and radio hosts and storytellers? How much did you need a role model when you were a kid? And did you really, truly have one?

A couple of weeks ago a young butch friend of mine asked me if I would help her out with her art school homework. She said she was doing a photo project, taking pictures of older butches. You know, like, documenting her elders.

Sure, I thought to myself, I know several older butches who I could hook her up with. A couple of them have moved to the sunshine coast like they do, but I could certainly track them down, no problem.

It slowly dawned on me that she was referring to me. I was the older butch she wanted to document. At first this realization made me laugh, and then it made my right knee ache like it does.

I am forty-three. She is twenty-one. I can't help but do the math. I had been out of the closet for three years already by the time she was born. I was navigating my way through the gender binary blues when she was learning to do up the Velcro straps on her first-day-of-school shoes. She has probably never dialed a rotary phone.

More and more at my shows, young butches and barely whiskered trans guys have been coming up and telling me that my books and stories helped them get through high school, or even junior high. They thank me for being a role model. This makes me feel simultaneously honoured and terrified. It makes my heart sing to know that they had what I didn't even know I needed when I was a kid: someone they could imagine growing up to be like. It makes my heart pound to know that this means I now have to somehow be worthy of this kind of respect.

How can I possibly be a role model, when I feel like I am just now starting to fit into my own skin? When I am still stretching and bending the space around me to make room for myself? How could I possibly give advice away when I just got my hands on it?

I find it is way easier to imagine whispering any wisdom I may have gleaned from the last four decades into the ear of a younger me. If I could magically tell my younger self something I know now that I wish I had known then, what would that be?

First of all, I would tell myself not to be too proud to ask for advice. Remember, you don't have to take advice just because someone has given it. Of course, my twenty-one-year-old self may not have taken the time to listen to present day me, but I will continue, regardless.

Dear younger self: floss your teeth. It turns out you will eventually be a working artist, just like you always dreamed. A man named Stephen Harper will one day rule this land, and he will care nothing for artists, or queers, or even health care. You need teeth, and you alone will be financially responsible for them. Floss is cheaper than even your commie pinko east end lesbian dentist will be.

Quit smoking. Please see above. I am not going to say this again. Okay, I am. Quit smoking right now.

Your mother is worried that no one will like you, or hire you, or even love you, if you look "like that." She is wrong. This next bit is really important: she does not mean to intentionally do you harm, or cause you to fear who and what you truly are. She worries because she fears what the world might do to you, and because she doesn't know any successful tattooed butch storytellers with biceps and a brush cut. Yet. But one day she will, and she is going to love the hell out of future you. Trust me on this one.

Do not cave into the pressure from mainstream society to fit in. You do not, and will not ever fit in. One day you will realize you don't even want to anymore, and that your difference is inherently tied to your beauty, and your bravery, and your giant, mystical, invisible brass balls. You will love these balls, and they will swing majestically between your ears, inside the head you will hold up proudly.

Do not cave into the pressure from the queer community to fit in, either. Make your own decisions, and trust your own heart. Being butch is not just a bus stop on the highway to transitioning. You will learn to love your butch self. If you do ever decide to go on testosterone, build yourself into a good man. The last thing the world needs is another misogynist prick. Be the man your father accidentally taught you to be, even if it was only because you didn't have a brother to help him out in the shop.

Make and keep long-term friendships. You will need them, and they will need you. This is one of the most important things you will ever do in your entire life.

Whenever possible, be polite. In the long run, your good manners will serve you better than even your most righteous rage.

Find a tailor, and be good to them. Get your pants hemmed properly, and learn what it feels like to have your clothes really fit your body. People come in all shapes, clothes do not. This is a wrong that can be easily righted. The world is going to try to squeeze you into many things that do not fit you, but your clothes need not be one of them.

Seek out a mentor. Listen to what they have to say, and then follow your own path. Keep a journal, because one day, someone is going to look up to you, and even ask you for advice, and you are going to wish you had taken better notes.

So go. Find yourself a mentor, and be a role model. Be a leader. Be the change we need to see. Don't wait for it to get better, make it better. Write us some better stories. Because somewhere, there is a kid out there who really needs your strength, and your courage. Someone out there needs you to be every bit of your brave, beautiful, fabulous, talented self.

Letter fr Grammar Wizard

From: Dark Princess
To: Ivan Coyote

Hello you probly get a lot of emails, so ill try to stay a bit to the point i guess... btw im the girl (Jamie) from the alternative school ... kinky switch omni sexual, with ptsd,panic attacks, bullyed from grade 4-12lvl5ish lol didnt really show up after sertian point., etc,.... anywho ...sence i was too nervous and over exausted to really speak during your time here on my oppyions on what i think should an dshould not be done about bullying I figured id email you. for one in the murphy centre there is a zero tolerence on bullying and i do personaly find it a safe conforting enviorment over all in terms of free expression etc. How ever.... i do believe in regular school systems they should be taught as a course senstivity training, basic psychology(aka how your actions effect people), how to comunicate your problems, and that it is truely ok to talk to a councolar about your issues.I do not believe everysingle bully is the way they are cause of issues i do believe that some sensitvity training , knowlage, and a good set of communicational skills might help someone who was prone to being a bully ... help in terms of lessining the way they do it etc... With that said i do not

187

think it will work for all but some it might ... sence that would be a big change a easyer to pass off way to explain it would be not only to show the person how it would effect someone , tell stories like you do, do, but mabye teach people that no one is allone, not the one doing the bullying nore the one being bullyed. As easy as it would be for me to hold hate toward thoes who did bully me the only feelings i allow my self is a will to try to over come everything... This is not perosnaly easy for me i do not think Growing a Thick skin is something people should be Fourced into doing at all i think it is something which should happen with maturity instead.I was bullyed physicaly, verbaly, mostly verbaly i was also psychologialy abused interms of the face my friends would be bullied till they told my secrets and stoped talkling to me anywho back to the view enough personal stories less you want to hear about it all if so feel free to ask i hav no problem telling you . I just find it a bit easyer for me if it alk about it. Back to ideas on how to stop it.I think understanding the person bullied(do not like to refer to them as a victum even tho some are i personaly do not like to view my self as one only because it would mean i had no control and in my eyes quitting school/ending it in someway was some fourm of control....)understanding them by seeing there prespective, what might be wrong thats making kids want to hurt them, if you can help sooth them in anyway what could you do, better councleing and tolerance /senstivity training for school staff members and even Students !!!!!!. Understanding the bully what makes someone bully , what kinds of ways can you help prevent bullies, is there anything you can do to help make a bully less likely to hurt anyone, school punishments like fourced tolerance class work, or senstivity classess, or even videos with tests on how to behave around people im sure after ENOUGH times doing it they will learn or get sick of it , of course also sending them to a guidance councolar before the principal might help as well.   Sorry this might be a bit overwalminin in terms of condenced info please email me back with in- sigh t questions etc.. or even conversation etc......

Five: Folks I Felt It Necessary to School in Some Way or Another, with Varying Degrees of Success

Judging a Book

There's an old cliché, something about how you can choose your friends but you can't choose your family. I travel a lot, and I'd like to add a line, or at least a footnote, about how you also can't choose who you sit next to on an airplane ride, especially if you're flying in economy class.

I am a collector of stories, and a connoisseur of characters, so for the most part I love the random way that travelling strangers enter and exit each other's lives. I relish the chance to spend a few hours listening to the life story of a little old lady who usually only talks to her cat or the postman, or the girl that her family hired to come and clean the house once a week, ever since her daughter got too busy with the twins and the promotion. I notice how thin her skin seems, stretched like tracing paper over the blue veins that map the backs of her hands. How they shake just a little when she holds up a photo for me to see, how she spills a little bit of sugar when she pours it from the tiny packet and has to hold her paper cup with both hands. I savour all these details, and save them as souvenirs. Some people take pictures or buy postcards to remember where they have been. I collect people, and conversations.

One time I spent three hours waiting for the fog to lift in San Francisco with a guy who told me that he spends so much time on the road he never fully unpacks his suit-case, and that he has missed nine of his son's twelve birth-day parties. He was a salesman who had single-handedly cornered the North American market for snow globes. His chest swelled proudly when he passed me his business card and announced that if I ever bought a quality snow globe anywhere on the continent, chances were it was one of his. Not the cheap ones, mind you, but the good kind, where the snow floats around for a while before it falls and collects on the bottom.

When he found out I was a writer, he told me he had spent the last ten years working on a novel, mostly at night in hotel rooms, and that when he finally retired, he was go-ing to take a screenwriting class.

"Maybe I'm a writer too," he told me. "You never know. Stranger things have happened."

I told him I thought everyone had at least 1,000 great stories to tell, but we have been taught to believe that only heroes or serial killers or rich people or crime scene inves-tigators live lives worth writing down. He rubbed his bald spot with one hand for a bit, like he was thinking about something he forgot to do, and took a deep breath.

That's when he blurted out that he hated his job, but the only thing he'd ever been better than everyone else at was selling snow globes, and that his wife hadn't touched him in three years, ever since he put on forty pounds after his back surgery, and he was pretty much convinced that she was banging his son's soccer coach and how the worst part was that he didn't even care anymore, but he didn't want to leave her because she would get the house, and he loved that house, and his dog, who had lived to be almost fifteen years old, was buried in the backyard right next to the apple tree, and what if his wife sold the house and bought a condo when the kids moved out so she wouldn't have to mow the lawn, and maybe a dead dog was a terrible reason to stay married to someone who won't look at you without a shirt on, but he was hardly ever home anyways, except for long weekends like this, and if the weather didn't get better he wouldn't make it home at all. Then he apologized and said he didn't know why he was telling me all this, that he hadn't even talked to his best friend about any of it, on account of how they worked for the same company, and getting too personal might put a strain on their business relationship. I hugged a perfect stranger that night because I knew his wife wouldn't, and I think of him now whenever I see snow that falls slowly.

Today I sat next to a man who immediately informed me that he was on his way to Europe to work with the Christian Embassy, spreading the good word of the Lord. Before the plane was off the ground, he asked me if I had a girlfriend. I took this line of inquiry to mean that he thought I was a clean-cut young man, and therefore possessed a soul worth saving. I told him the truth; I did have a girlfriend, and no, we were not married yet, and yes, we were indeed living together, and yes, I was aware that we were living in sin. I smiled inside at just how much sin he didn't realize we were actually living in, and pondered telling him I was not as nice, young, or male as he appeared to think I was.

Then I realized how fun it was to listen to a fundamentalist Christian lecture me on how God wanted me to marry my girlfriend, how the family unit in this country was depending on me, and how not fun it might immediately become if he were to find out he was brushing thighs with a full-blown sodomite disguised as a harmless wayward Catholic boy in a crisp shirt and a tie. I knew there was as much chance of me changing his mind about anything as there was that he would ever lead me back to the path of righteousness, so I told him he was right, and that I was going to propose to my girlfriend as soon as I had enough money saved up to buy her a decent conflict-free diamond ring. He took this to mean that he had helped me see the light, and continued the Lord's work all the way to Toronto. When the plane finally landed, he shook my hand and told me that I seemed like a good person, and that if I were ever in Guelph, I should look up his son, who had strayed from God's path a little and had pierced his eyebrow and was pursuing an arts degree.

"I'd like him to meet some friends with ambition. People who realize that appearances matter. I pray that he grows up to be just like you."

"I hope God answers that prayer," I told him. "I really do."

Take That

I had a forty-five minute layover in Ottawa, on my way to Halifax. I was halfway through my complimentary newspaper when I heard them arrive at the gate. Forty teenage girls and their thirty-something male chaperone were getting on the plane with me. The chaperone was one of those cool teachers, we all had one at some point, the kind who teaches gym or band and sports a ponytail and over-manicured facial hair. He's the kind of guy who buffs his nails and lets the kids call him by his first name, which is usually Steve or Rick or Darryl. Maybe he smokes a little pot on the weekends, too, and plays a little acoustic guitar. He wears designer jeans and tight t-shirts that show off his well-muscled forearms. The girls all harbour not-so-secret crushes on him, because, you know, he like totally understands them, plus he's handsome. The guys have more mixed emotions, a combination of wanting to be him and wanting to kill him, or at least one day beat him in an arm-wrestle. He calls everybody "buddy" or "kiddo."

Steve or Rick or Darryl clapped his hands together to get the girls' attention. "Okay, ladies, let's line up, and have your ID ready. Don't leave your garbage behind; let's make a positive impression here, okay? Make sure you have your buddy with you."

I buried my face in my newspaper. I've never been over-
ly fond of teenage girls, especially in packs, even when I
was attempting to be one. They're a mean, judgmental lot, I
find, and they still intimidate me. They whisper, they gawk,
and they snicker. It takes me back, I can't help it.
F.H. Collins High School in the early eighties was
ruled by her highnesses Wendy, Tracy, Sandra, Jeanie, and
Kerri-Anne. It was a time of big hair, small sweaters, and
tight jeans. All five girls possessed all of these prerequi-
sites. Their affections were highly sought after, and fleet-
ing. They liked me once for half a day when they found out
I was vaguely related by marriage to Jimmy Baker, my dad's
brother's wife's little brother, because he was cute, and had
his own car. But I soon fell from their favour over my in-
ability to grow breasts or like Depeche Mode.

At least they just pretended I didn't exist after that. It
could have been a lot worse. Ask "Pizza-Face'" Andrea Mullen or "Big-Fat" Alice Byers just how bad it could get.

Not much has changed since then. The jeans cover even
less skin, and the hair is a lot smaller, but the Wendys, Tra-
cys, Sandras, Jeanies, and Kerri-Annes still rule the school,
and I was getting on a plane with forty of them.

Everything was cool until I had to get up and go pee.
The girls were all sitting at the back of the plane. The bev-
erage cart was parked in the aisle two or three rows from
the bathrooms. I was going to have to wait in line and be
scrutinized by forty teenage girls.

My early teenage girl trauma was later complicated and
compounded by the fact that I am often mistaken by them

for a young man of appropriate cruising age. From eighteen rows away, I must have looked cute enough to check out. She had long, straight, copper-coloured hair and perfect skin and teeth. I disliked her immediately, just on principle. She fixed her blue eyes on me and elbowed her friend in the ribs. I pretended to be fascinated by my thumbnail and hated myself for caring about what I knew was going to happen next. Ten rows away, all three girls held their heads together and giggled, still trying to catch my eye.

But five rows away, the redhead peeled her lashes back from her eyes and sat up straight. She dropped her magazine and gripped her armrests in horror. Her mouth gaped open. She stared shamelessly at me, and then leaned over and covered her face in her hands. Her girlfriends leaned in to see what was the matter. She whispered something to them and they plastered their mouths with their palms. The redhead made pretend gagging motions.

I was right beside them now, and could hear them.

"That is the grossest thing I've seen all year. Oh my God, what is it? Does it have boobs? You look. No, I'm not looking, I feel totally sick. You check, Colleen, you were the one who thought he was cute. Was not. Were too. Oh my God, I can't tell what it is."

My face and ears were on fire. Did they think I couldn't hear them? I calmly put my right hand on the seat back in front of them and leaned into their row. I placed one word in front of the other, in an orderly fashion.

"Why don't you just ask *it* what it is? Maybe *it* is a human being with ears, and feelings. Why don't you just ask *it* what *it* is? Maybe *it* can talk, too, and maybe *it* will tell you. Go ahead, ask *it*. Because *it* is standing right here."

They just stared straight ahead, wordless. They pretended I wasn't there, like I didn't exist.

I splashed cold water on my face in the tiny bathroom. I thought about finding Steve or Rick or Darryl and telling him that his girls had failed to leave a positive impression here. Then I decided against it. I didn't feel like explaining myself, or receiving a forced, toe-kicking teenage apology.

The girls were still whispering mercilessly as I walked past them. They fell silent when they saw me. My hands were shaking. I hoped they couldn't see that.

I'd calmed myself down by the time the plane landed. I don't like standing up and waiting in the aisle while some guy way up in first class drags his laptop down from the overhead compartment and puts his jacket on in slow motion, all the while holding up the entire disembarking process, so I usually stay in my seat reading until almost everyone is off the plane.

I caught a flash of red hair in my periphery. I swear I didn't think about it. It wasn't planned. I sent no conscious signal to my leg to move, but just as Colleen passed my seat, my foot shot out and tripped her, all on its own. She fell perfectly, knocking over the two girls in front of her as well. The girl behind her tripped over the resulting tangle, and all four of them went down.

The blonde in the striped bell-bottoms leaped up first. "Jesus, Colleen, watch where you're going. I could have chipped a tooth. I just got my braces off."

199

They righted themselves and left the plane without looking back. I don't think even Colleen knew what I had done.

I sat in my aisle seat, shaking my head at myself. Good thing the two nice old ladies who had been seated next to me had already gotten off the plane, or they would have thought I had cruelly tripped an innocent sixteen-year-old girl with absolutely no provocation.

I tried to feel guilty. I tried to feel ashamed of my behaviour. I was an adult, I told myself, and I should have known better.

But I couldn't. I thought of Andrea Mullen, who is a lawyer now. I thought of Alice Byers, who overdosed on sleeping pills in her third year of university.

I smiled to myself. Take that, Wendy, Tracy, Sandra, Jeanie, and Kerri-Anne. Truth is, I never liked you guys anyways.

Bully This

I returned home from doing my anti-bullying storytelling show in a couple of small towns just in time to open the newspaper and read about right-wing Christian radio hosts and rogue school board members targeting programs like Out in Schools, and "pro-family" organizations taking out full-page ads full of hate and fear-mongering in national publications.

I had just performed for 1,500 kids in two days in four schools, and as always, I walked away feeling inspired and full of hope for the world. These kids are smarter and savvier than those on the right seem willing or able to give them credit for, and they are certainly wiser and worldlier than I remember being when I was fifteen.

That's the funny thing: that the evangelicals are so convinced that their kids will grow up heterosexual as long as they never cross paths with a living, breathing homosexual. It is like they actually believe that if they can somehow just keep us homos out of schools, or at least keep us in the closet, and keep our lives and our language out of the curriculum, that all of their children will magically grow up to be straight. What they forget is that no matter what kind of self-hatred and misinformed poison they whisper into their kids' ears, an estimated ten percent of them will grow up to be some sort of queer, and that the real question is whether they will somehow find the strength to survive and thrive and live truthfully despite what they were taught to believe about themselves.

So in some ways, every time I swallow the lump in my throat and step through those streaky glass doors at the front of every high school I enter, I am there for those kids the most. Because I know that despite how scary high school can be for some kids, for others high school is the only place they might have any hope of acceptance and support, because they are not going to find it at home.

The thing is, I don't even say the word queer while I am there. I just tell stories. Stories about growing up with my cousins and little sister, stories about my Gran. Stories about Wendy, Tracy, Sandra, Jeanie, and Kerri-Anne, the mean girls back at my own high school. My show is designed to get the kids talking about bullies and teen suicide and how the way we treat each other impacts the kind of people we are, and the kind of adults we might become. I don't need to say the word queer, because it is not about being queer. It is about each and every one of them feeling safe enough to access their education, and about respecting difference.

Because I remember who got picked on in school. The fat kids, the dumb kids, the slow kids, the fast kids, the poor kids, the boys who threw like girls, the kids who weren't white, the quiet kids, the religious kids. That's right, Christian right: your kids. The ones who weren't allowed to go on dates, go to dances, wear makeup or the right clothes, watch the right television shows, or listen to the right music. When I was in school, the most risqué show on TV was *Dallas* and the dangerous band was Judas Priest; today, maybe it is more like *True Blood* and Gaga, but the song remains the same.

I got this email when I got home, from one of the teachers: "We have had a two-year leadership focus on inclusiveness and anti-bullying and your presentation supported this so beautifully ... getting to that part of the audience that may not always be listening or be open to receiving a message. This week we had three different groups come up to our admin to report an incident where a vulnerable grade 10 boy was being harassed by older boys in the lounge. Our principal called all six of the boys up for a visit. They were banned from the lounge for a week and the public shaming was a lovely thing. Two of the boys called in were not harassing the boy, but they didn't say anything. They apologized for not speaking up when they knew they should have and could have stopped the ugly affair. Anyway, we think that your performance may have been fresh on our students' minds and something very good came out of a potentially very bad situation. So thank you again."

I also want to share part of a letter I got from a student after a show I did in a high school last spring:

"Heeeyyy. So you came to my school today. After I got in the car with my older brother and told him all about you, and he goes, Britney, you are one of those girls. I yelled at him and then gave him the silent treatment the whole way back, but when I wasn't talking to him I was thinking yah, I am one. I'm a Kerri-Anne or a Wendy or that volleyball team. But I don't want to be. So I just wanted to say thanks. Because even though I have all this respect for you, I don't always give that respect to other people, and I know I am not going to change this second cause it's been a part of me since I can remember, but I'm going to be conscious of it all the time now. I know you are making an impact I just wanted to be the extra email that helps motivate you to never quit."

So, Britney, I promise you, I will never quit. And evangelicals, you might want to think again about stopping folks like me from doing this kind of work in schools. Because chances are pretty good that it might just be your kid who is going to need us to be there for them the most.

Imagine a Pair of Boots

Imagine a pair of boots. A sturdy, well-made, kind of nondescript pair of boots. They are functional enough, but kind of plain. Imagine that you live in a country where every citizen is issued this one pair of boots at birth, and that there are no other footwear options permitted by law. If you grow out of or wear through the soles of these government-issued boots, you may trade them in for a new pair, always identical to your old ones. Imagine that everyone you know wears these very same boots without question or complaint.

Now imagine that your right foot is two sizes bigger than your left one. That no matter what you do, one boot will chafe and the other will slip, and both will cause blisters. When you mention your discomfort you are told that odd-sized pairs of boots are forbidden, because they cause confusion and excess paperwork. It is explained to you that this footwear system works perfectly for everyone else, and reminded that there are people in other countries who have no boots at all. You are beat up in grade three because none of the other kids have ever seen feet like yours. The teacher tells you that you should probably just learn to keep your boots on. Your parents blame each other. You end up wearing an extra sock on your small foot to compensate, and never go to swimming pools. Your feet sweat profusely in the summer and you always undress in the dark. You hate your feet but need them to walk and stand up on. You hate your boots even more. You dream of things that look like sandals and moccasins, but you have no words for them. You learn things will be easier for you if you just never talk about your feet. One time on the bus, you spot a guy with the exact same limp as you, but you pretend not to see him. He watches you limp off at your bus stop and then looks the other way. You can't stop thinking about the man with the limp for weeks. You are nineteen years old and until that day on the bus you thought you were the only person in the country who couldn't fit into their boots.

I have always felt this way about gender pronouns, that 'she' pinches a little and 'he' slips off me too easily. I'm often asked by well-intentioned people which pronoun I prefer, and I always say the same thing: that I don't really have a preference, that neither pronoun really fits, but thank you for asking, all the same. Then I tell them they can call it like they see it, or mix it up a little if they wish. Or, they can try to avoid using he or she altogether. I suggest this even though I am fully aware of the fact it is almost impossible to talk about anything other than yourself or inanimate objects without using a gender-specific pronoun. It is especially hard at gigs, when the poor host has to get up and introduce me to the audience. No matter which pronoun the host goes with, there is always someone cringing in the crowd, convinced that an uncomfortable mistake has just been made. I know it would be easier if I just picked a pronoun and stuck with it, but that would be a compromise made for the comfort of everyone else but me. A decision that would inevitably leave me with a blister, or even a nasty rash. Perfect strangers have been asking me if I am a boy or a girl as far back as I can remember. Not all of them are polite about it. Some are just curious, others ask me like they have every right to know, as if my ambiguity is a personal insult to their otherwise completely understandable reality. Few of them seem to realize they have just interrupted my day to demand I give someone I don't know personal information they don't really need to sell me a movie ticket or a newspaper. I have learned the hard way to just answer the question politely, so they don't think I'm rude. In my braver days, when someone asked if I was a boy or a girl, I would say something flip and witty, like 'yes' or 'no' or 'makes you wonder, doesn't it?,' but I found that this type of tactic greatly increased the chances I would get the living shit kicked out of me, so I eventually knocked it off. Then I went through a phase where I would answer calmly, and then casually ask them something equally as personal, such as did they have chest hair or were they satisfied with the size of their penis or were those their real breasts, just so they would see how it felt, but this proved just as ineffective.

A couple of months ago, as I was smoking outside the Anza Club in Vancouver after a gig, this young guy marched up and interrupted the person I was talking with to ask me if I was a man or a woman. I told him I was a primarily estrogen-based organism, and then I asked him the exact same question. He took two steps back and dropped his jaw. "I'm a man." He seemed visibly shaken by the thought of any other option.

"And were you just born male?" I continued, winking at my companion.

"Well, yeah, of course I was."

"How interesting." I lit another smoke.

"Hard to tell these days," my friend chimed in.

The guy walked off, looking confused and kind of vulnerable.

"He's gone home to grow a moustache," my buddy said, then laughed and shook his head.

I thought about it all later, how the guy's ego had crumpled right in front of us, just because a stranger had questioned his masculinity. How scared he was of not being a real man, how easy it had been to take him down. It dawned on me that if you've never had a blister, then you'll never have a callus, either. And if your soles are too soft, then you are screwed if you ever lose your boots.

Bathroom Chronicles

Lately, I find myself on the road a lot. Sleeping in beds un-
familiar with the shape of me, feeling along strange walls
to find the light switch in the dark, waking up to wonder at
a ceiling I've never seen before in the daylight of a different town. Wearing the same pair of pants for a week and
running my fingers over a calling card in my pocket when
I miss my girlfriend. Airports and a highway and little tiny
soaps and MapQuest and gas stations. Always gas stations.
Because no matter where you are, or how much time you
have until you have to be somewhere else, you're going to
need gas, and someone always has to pee.

For me, the best gas station bathroom scenario is the
single stall version with the sturdy locking door with a sign
on it that says men-slash-women and you don't have to ask
for the key first. These are the bathrooms most conducive
to a stress-free urination experience for me, for a number of
reasons. First of all, you don't need to ask for the key. The
key for the gas station bathroom is usually somewhat wet for
some reason, which I find unsanitary and disturbing, and is
invariably tied or chained to a filthy germ-harbouring item
which is hard to pocket or lose, such as a piece of hockey
stick, a giant spoon, or a tire iron. You have to ask for the
key from the either bored or harried and always underpaid

guy behind the counter, and if there are two keys, one for the men's and another for the women's, then the cashier has either no time if there's a line-up, or lots of time if things are slow, to decide for himself which key he should give you. Keep in mind that he is probably feeling unfulfilled about the fact that he is ten times more likely to be robbed at gunpoint than he is to get a raise anytime in the near future, and that deciding which washroom he thinks I should be using is the most arbitrary power he's been afforded by this job since he caught that twelve-year-old shoplifting condoms and decided not to call the cops because at least the kid was stealing responsibly.

So this is the guy who gets to decide where I get to pee. I have learned that asking for the key to a specific washroom will only increase the odds that he will notice that the washroom I wish to enter doesn't match the hair or voice or footwear of the person he sees in front of him. Maybe he couldn't care less which bathroom I use, maybe his favourite sister is a dyke. But maybe his religion tells him I am damned, maybe him and his buddies almost killed a guy once for wearing a pink shirt, just in case he was a queer, just for fun. Maybe he dreamt of kissing his best friend all the way through grade eight but never did, and he hates me because I remind him of how scared he is of his own insides. I cannot know his mind. I am in a strange town, and something about me doesn't fit. It is best if I let him decide, and don't draw attention, or alert anyone in the line-up behind me to his conundrum.

Maybe you think I'm just paranoid, that I'm a drama

queen, or that I exaggerate to make a point. I would say good for you, that your gender or skin colour or economic status has allowed you to feel safe enough that you still think the rest of us are making this stuff up. You probably don't even realize how lucky you are to be able to not believe me when I tell you that every time I have to pee in a public bathroom, I also take a risk that someone will take issue with me being somewhere they believe to be the wrong room, depending on who they mistook me to be, based solely on that first quick glance.

I can pray for a wheelchair-accessible stall, or one of the ungendered kind with a baby-changing station in it, and then hope that no one is waiting there when I slip out, able-bodied and childless. I can cross my fingers that the ladies' room is empty, or bolt quietly for the closest empty stall if it is not. Unfortunately, women and children have many good reasons to fear what they think is a man in their washroom. I have learned to be more forgiving of their concern, and try not to take any hostility too personally. They only want the same thing I'm looking for: a safe place to pull down their pants and pee.

I can hold my nose and use the men's room, and if I'm lucky there will be a seat on the toilet and the guy who comes in to use the urinal will not be the type who hates slightly effeminate men, or the type who likes them a little too much. In men's rooms, I squat and pee quickly, simulta-neously relieved and terrified when I am alone.

Over the years I have learned a few techniques, like not drinking pop in movie theatres and holding my pee for probably unhealthy lengths of time. I do my best to be polite and non-confrontational, even when confronted or questioned rudely. One of my favourite methods is to enter the women's room with a preferably ladylike companion who has been previously instructed to ask me if I have a tampon in my purse. I answer her in the most demure and feminine tone I can muster that I left my purse in the car, or that I'm down to my last pantyliner, and dash for the first open stall.

Just recently, I accidentally improvised the perfect line to deliver to the nice but confused lady that I often meet on my way out of the gas station bathroom. She was standing with her hand on the half-open door, looking first at me and then again at the sign that said "Women" on it. She was in her later sixties, and I felt bad that I had startled her, or maybe made her feel even for a moment that she was lost, or in the men's room, where she might not be safe. That I had scared an old woman with a full bladder. Again.

"It's okay," I smiled and said calmly. "It's just me."

Dear Lady in the Women's Washroom

I can only surmise from our recent interaction that I startled you in the women's washroom at the mall today. I guess I don't look much like what you seem to think a female washroom user should. This is not the first time this has happened to me; in fact, this was not the first time this has happened to me this week. Forgive me if I was not as patient with you as you seemed to feel I should have been, but I would like to point out that your high pitched squeal startled me, and I needed to urinate very badly. Perhaps I was not as gracious as I could have been.

To ensure that the next time this happens to you, or me, things go more smoothly for everyone involved, I have jotted down a couple of notes for your reference.

Not everyone fits easily into one of the two options provided on your standard public washroom doors. In my world, gender is a spectrum, not a binary. Just because an individual does not present as what you feel a woman should look like, does not mean that they do not belong there. Public washrooms are just that: public. This means that you do not get to decide whom you share them with. I would like to remind you that everyone, regardless of their gender identity or presentation, needs to pee.

213

For some of us, public washrooms are stressful places. We generally avoid them whenever possible. Please, rest assured that if I have chosen to enter a public washroom in spite of my long and arduous history with them, that I have taken the time to carefully note which door I am about to walk into, and that I am confident I have chosen the lesser of two evils. I am, in fact, hyper aware of which bathroom I am in. It is not necessary for you to stare at me, pointedly refer to the graphic on the door, or discuss my decision loudly with your companions. Gawking, elbowing your friend, and repeatedly clearing your throat are also not helpful. Trust me, I will be in and out as quick as is humanly possible.

The next time this happens to you, I would like you to think twice before screaming. I would like you to imagine what it feels like to be me. Imagine being screeched at by a perfect stranger. Now imagine being screeched at when you really need to pee, or your tampon gave out twenty minutes ago. Sucks, doesn't it?

I want you to know that I understand wanting to feel safe from men while using the bathroom in a public place. This is, in fact, the primary reason I don't just use the other bathroom. That, and I have a very delicate sense of smell, and don't like returning filthy toilet seats to the down position.

I also would like you to know that trans and gender queer people suffer from many more bladder infections, urinary tract issues, and general pee-related health problems than the general population. I humbly ask you to consider why this might be the case.

I would also like you to know that I have had the great pleasure of spending time with a seven-year-old and an eight-year-old tomboy lately. Both young girls have experienced serious bullying at school and day camp over their gender presentation, especially in and around the question of gendered bathrooms. They have both come home from school in tears, and one of them even quit science camp because of it. Hearing that these two sweet, kind, amazing children have both already experienced "the bathroom problem" that I so often face myself not only broke my heart, it enraged me. I feel that this type of bullying has impeded their ability to access a public education, and impacted their desire to participate in valuable activities outside of school as well. I would like you to consider how this might affect their self-esteem, their grades, and their sense of self-worth. I remind you that they are just little kids. They are only in elementary school, and it has started already. Not such a little thing after all, is it?

I ask you to forgive me my impatience with you at the mall today. But how could I possibly not think of my two little friends, and feel anything but rage?

See, when you scream at me without thinking in the women's washroom, you are implicating yourself in a rigid, two-party gender system that tells others that it is okay to discriminate against people like me. Even little children who are like me. This is the very same attitude that results in queer youth suicides, and high school murderers being acquitted because the dead boy asked for it by wearing a skirt and makeup. It is this same attitude that turns its head when trans women are shot at by off duty police officers, and denied services at women's shelters. It is this kind of sentiment that says it is okay to deny us housing, or a job, or the right to adopt children or dance on a freaking reality television show. If you think I am making any of this up, then I encourage you to open up your newspaper and have another look.

I would like to remind you that this very same two-party gender system is enforced on me and others like me everyday, policed by people just like you. It starts very young, and sometimes is subtle, as small as a second look on the way out of a bathroom stall, but sometimes it is deafening, and painful, and violent, even murderous.

So, the next time you meet up with someone like me in the 'ladies room,' please think twice before screaming. I am not there by accident. In fact, I spent a lot more time looking at the sign on the door than you ever have.

Truth Story

A couple of years ago I was backstage at a little music festival with my friend and guitar player, Richard. It was a breezy blue-skied July day, drawing quite a decent crowd for a small town. I pulled back the velvet curtain a crack to have a sneak peek at our audience. The entire first row was a beefy, bleeding, tattooed wall of biker-looking types. I swallowed and pulled the curtain back.

"Rico ..." I whispered. "I think we're gonna have to change up our set a little. I think maybe we need to drop the Francis story and do the fishing story instead."

The Francis story was a tale about a little boy who liked to wear dresses. I thought maybe a less faggy, more fishing-oriented piece might go over a little better with this crowd.

Richard took a deep breath and gave me his I-am-about-to-tell-you-something-for-your-own-good look.

"First of all," he began, "the truck is parked right backstage. Second, artists are always allowed to talk about stuff that other people would get punched out for bringing up, remember? It's part of the deal."

I nodded, because this was true. Richard inhaled again, obviously not finished yet.

"But most important of all is, don't be a chicken, Coyote. Have some balls. What, you only going to tell that story to people who don't need to hear it?"

"You bastard." I smiled at him.

He shrugged. He knew me. Knew what to say to activate my stubborn streak.

The biggest and most bad-assed-looking of the bikers stood there in the front row, his veiny forearms crossed over his black t-shirt, for the first ten minutes of my set. He even laughed here and there, the skin around his eyes crinkling into well-worn crow's feet every time he smiled. I started to relax a little, and when I started the first couple of lines of the Francis story, Richard tipped his head in my direction in approval and played like an angel beside me.

Halfway through the story, I watched the gigantic man in the front row start to unpeel himself right in front of me. First he uncrossed his arms and let them fall to his sides. Then he bit his lower lip, and his handlebar moustache began to quiver a little. By the end, he was crying giant man-sized tears, unabashedly letting them roll down his dusty cheeks and disappear into his beard. He almost got me choked up too, just watching him. I was used to the drag queens losing it in the last couple of paragraphs of the Francis story, but this was something else altogether.

After, when Richard and I were loading gear into the back of his pick-up, I looked up and he was standing next to the table that held the cheese trays and the juice cooler, waiting to talk to me.

He rushed toward me and picked me right up off the ground in a cigar-scented hug. When he let me back down to the ground, he still held both of my hands in his baseball glove-sized hands, squeezing them until it almost hurt.

"I just had to thank you. Just had to tell you how much that story you told meant to me." He pulled me up close to him, and lowered his voice a couple of decibels. "My baby brother James died from AIDS, ten years ago tomorrow. My only brother. I loved him like crazy when we were kids, but my dad ... well ... let's just say the old man wasn't very flexible in his beliefs about certain things. He never understood Jamie, right from the get-go, and Christ, he was hard on the kid. Beat the living shit out of him one time when he caught him wearing my sister Donna's lipstick. Finally kicked him out when Jamie was fifteen. Nobody knew, back then, and by the time we did, it was too late. I never stuck up for him, never said a word, and to this day I have never forgiven myself for it. My baby brother, out on the street. How else was he going to get by? He was only a kid."

He looked me right in the eyes. By this time, both of us were crying.

"He was the sweetest fucking kid in the world. Your little friend in that story reminded me of James. There were five of us kids, but he was always my mom's favourite. The old man blamed her, said she babied him, but we all knew he was just born like that. That was just who he always was." He cleared his throat and wiped his eyes on the hair on the back of his hands. Looked a bit sheepish all of a sudden. "Anyways, just wanted to thank you for that. Good stuff."

Then he shook my hand and was gone. I've never forgotten him, and I imagine him standing behind me whenever I find myself scared of the next story I am about to tell, or afraid of the people I'm about to tell it to.

Last week I walked into a classroom at the college in Powell River, to tell stories to a bunch of Adult Education students. Working-class town, working-class guys all lined up in the back row. I found myself wishing with my whole heart I had not chosen to wear a paisley dress shirt that morning. What was I thinking?

Then I took a deep breath and told them a story. I started with the one about my dad. The one where I had almost given up wishing he would quit drinking, but then one day he did. Afterward, this guy with biceps the size of my thighs came up and thanked me. He had sleeve tattoos and could barely squeeze his muscles into his white Stanfield crewneck.

"I really liked the one about your dad," he explained. "I could totally relate to him. I used to be a welder, too."

Six: Wisdom I Found, Learned or Was Given

My Dad Told Me

It was a Friday afternoon, sunny and lazy. I ran into my friend Sir coming out of her apartment building, and we went for a coffee. She grabbed a table outside on the deck in the warm sun and I went inside for two Americanos.

I squeezed past the lady in the hippie dress and sat beside Sir and her cowboy hat, across from two biker types and their overfilled ashtray. Sir passed me a piece of the newspaper.

"Business section?" I asked her. "What am I gonna do with this? Check my stocks?" She passed me the New Homes section, smiling. "Smart ass," I said. "At least give me the Local News bit. Don't make me roll up Fashion and pummel you with it."

She passes me the front page. A true friend, indeed.

"It's not the same as inside," the bigger of the two bikers laments. "Inside there is a code, you know, a way of being that makes sense ... then when you get out ..."

"It's an adjustment," his buddy nods. "Took me over a year to be able to sleep past six a.m. Ate pork chops every Tuesday for a while, until I got used to Tuesday isn't pork chop night for the whole planet. You've only been out a coupla weeks. It gets better. When's your kid gonna be here?"

"Ten after."

The second guy stands, extends his hand. Slaps the other guy on the shoulder. They half-hug, awkward. "So I'll make a move, leave you to it. Take care, buddy. Same time, next week?"

My face is hidden behind pictures of Iraqi prisoners. I can't face the news; instead I am eavesdropping on a rare bonding moment between these two men. I sneak a peek at Sir. She is watching the second man disappear around the corner; his wallet is wearing through the denim of his right back pocket, the chain swinging, smokes, cell phone, and truck keys in hand. The sound of his boots on pavement fades with him. She smiles at me. We were both witness.

A tall, pimply boy gets off the bus and crosses the street. He squints into the sun, holds up a knuckly hand across his eyes. He jumps over the guardrail and slumps into the empty chair. He is all right angles and straight lines. His feet seem impossibly big in brand new white runners. One shin is road-rashed and picked.

The biker leans across the table to hug him, the kid moves to meet him and knocks over a half-empty bottle of apple juice. His father catches it before it hits the table.

"Sorry, Dad."

His dad smiles and surveys the boy. "You look great. I think you're finally taller than your father."

"By three-quarters of an inch." The boy raises his eyebrows and grins.

"Your mom?" Dad is staring at his fingernails.

"She's good. You staying at Uncle John's?"

"For a while. I'm looking at a place this weekend. There's

a skatepark a block away. I'm getting a pull-out couch for you."

They talk like this for a while. I'm smoking and getting involved in the sorry state of the planet, enough so I'm almost not eavesdropping anymore, until I hear the man ask his kid if he's having any luck with the ladies.

The kid swallows, his oversize Adam's apple plunging in discomfort. He shakes his head. "There was that one chick from Kelowna, remember? She was staying at her Grandma's? That was a while ago ..."

"That was last summer, little dude. School's almost out again."

"Yeah, well, I'm not like you. Girls don't like me too much, mostly. I don't have the magic touch like you."

"It's not a magic touch. You want to know my secret? My fail-proof method?"

The kid leans forward. Behind my newspaper, I find I have leaned forward too. Sir has cocked her head, too. We are all waiting.

"Let me just grab myself another coffee, and I'll tell you all about it. Hold that thought. You still drinking iced tea?"

The kid nods. His dad gets up and goes inside. All three of us sit back, impatient. I watch him make his way back to our table. Average height. Over-size biceps. Bleeding tattoos. Not an ugly man by any stretch, but, as my aunts would say, nothing to write home about. He resumes his seat, lights an Export 'A', and stirs his coffee with a hand that makes the spoon look like it came from an Easy-Bake Oven Set.

"Where were we?"

"You were going to tell me how to meet chicks."

"Right. I'll tell you the one thing that women cannot resist in a man. The one thing that will always keep them coming back for more."

For the love of Christ, spit it out already, man, I'm thinking. *We all need to know here.*

"Listen to them."

The kid sits up straight with a sideways glance.

"I mean, really listen. Ask her about how her day went. Be interested. Don't just act that way, I mean really be interested in her. What she has to say, what she thinks about things."

"And then ...?"

"That's it, son. That's all. You'd be surprised how many guys never figure that one out, but that's it. My big secret. Really listen to her, and then if you're lucky, when you come home from work, there will be a good woman there. Cooking for her every once in a while never hurt a guy in the long run, either."

The kid looks at his father. I look at Sir. Sir looks at the biker, then she meets my eyes. Again, we were both witness.

The biker drains his coffee. "C'mon, kiddo, I'll buy you a slice."

The two of them stand up and walk together down the block—noisy black Dayton boots and silent white runners, respectively.

Sir is shaking her head, smiling. "That was just about the sweetest thing I ever heard. Did you get all that?" she asks me.

I nod reverently.

For the first time, the lady in the hippie dress lowers her paperback and speaks up, her eyes moist and bright blue. "Now if only someone would have told my husband that, I might still own half of that cabin on Salt Spring Island."

Spare Change

Corner of Pender and Abbott, just before midnight. Whose bright idea was it to build a multiplex theatre and high-end mall here? Remember when it was a parking lot? I think I liked it better as a pit filled with water. I knew a guy who was arrested once for canoeing in the flooded hole that gaped where this mall now is.

I light a smoke into cupped palms. Orange glows bright, then dimmer.

Streetlights leak shifting spilled paint reflections off shining sidewalks and pavement. It is chilly tonight, like this evening belongs in a whole different month than the rest of this week.

I smoke with one hand and run fingertips over the ridged edges of quarters in my pocket with the other.

There's a woman, she's just rounded the corner off Carrall onto Pender Street, she's walking towards me. Her dress has two straps; one has fallen to her elbow and remains there, the other clings to a prominent collarbone. I watch her only because there is nobody else on the street to look at. She shuffles along the sidewalk, fists blossoming into five narrow fingers and then closing again. Repeat. Eyes down, back and forth, she searches the sidewalk and gutter. She scoops up a flat cigarette butt and places it into the shapeless front pocket of her dress. A small baggie is picked up, opened, sniffed, licked, and dropped again. She runs a yellow tongue over peeling lips, passes a sleeveless wrist under her nose. Repeat.

I look down as she starts to get close to me. I can hear the sound of her flip-flops sucking and slapping against the wet pavement. The sound stops in front of me. I don't look up. Both hands are in my pockets. My half-smoked cigarette is crushed and soggy, an inch away from the toe of my boot. *What a waste*, I think. Too late to fix it.

"Spare some change, young fella?" Her voice is deeper than her small frame seems capable of.

I shake my head.

She lifts one lip a little, in my direction. "I know you've got change in your pockets. I can hear it. Heard it all the way up the street."

"You asked me if I could spare some change, not if I had any."

She raises her eyebrows. They have been plucked and then painted back on, but she raises them nonetheless. "We got a wise guy, huh?" She flips then flops back two steps and surveys me closer. "You go to college? Because that, my friend, is lawyer talk."

I shake my head. "I'm a writer. I tell stories."

She snorts. "Same diff. Makin' shit up. Twisting the facts so they end up on your side. I'll ask you again, counsellor. Can I have some of the change I can hear in your pocket?"

"It's not change. It's my car keys." I jingle them for evidence. *Exhibit A.*

"Other pocket. Nice try. What, are you afraid I'll go spend your hard-earned money on drugs?"

I half-shrug, half-nod. "What if I get you something to eat?" I motion over my shoulder to the McDonald's behind me, which is getting ready to close up.

She snorts again. "That garbage? Now, that stuff will kill you."

We both laugh. I pull my other hand out of my pocket. Two loonies, a twoonie, three quarters. I hand it over. A nicotine-stained hand shoots out and collects. The change disappears before I can squeeze out a second thought. She doesn't thank me.

"You're welcome," I say.

"What? You want me to thank you now? I took your money to make you feel better about having more of it than me. I just did you a favour, if you think about it. Don't you feel like a better person now, helping out an old woman? I'm the mother of four children. I have three grandchildren. I'm almost sixty-five years old."

"You don't look a day over eighty," I quip.

"Why, thank you."

We laugh again, she coughs.

"Where are your kids, then?"

"My kids? Where are my kids? You mean why don't my kids swoop down and rescue their poor old mother from the mean streets of the Downtown Eastside?"

"Well, yeah I guess that's pretty much what I mean."

"And argue over whose turn it is to keep me in their basement suite? All the free cable I can watch? I tried that. There's one catch. There's always the one catch."

"What's that?"

"I'm never allowed to bring my heroin."

I nod, because there seems to be nothing to say.

"Shit happens, kiddo. Sometimes life gets in the way of all your plans. I'm too old to live under someone else's roof, someone else's laws. Had enough of that when I was married to the bastard, may he rest in peace." She makes the sign of the cross in the air with her right hand and falls silent for a bit.

I nod again and reach into my pocket for my smokes. I offer her one, light both.

She inhales deeply, stares at the red end of her cigarette. "It's the simple things. Tell you what—how 'bout you spare me a couple more of these for later?"

I look down into my pack. There are two left.

"I'd offer to buy them from you, but you'd probably just go spend the money on more cigarettes." She smiles, raises one eyebrow, and then winks at me.

I hand her the rest of the package. Up close, she smells like rose water.

"There now." The pack disappears. She pats my forearm. "Doesn't that feel better?"

My Kind of Guy

I am good at finding my kind of place for breakfast. Especially in small towns. This place had all the right elements: it was embedded in the middle of a mini mall, in between a second-hand furniture store and a laundromat. Lots of new pick-ups parked outside. All-you-can-eat Chinese buffet on Sunday nights. All-day breakfast for five bucks. Neon open sign flashing in the window. Vinyl booths and chrome-edged tables that have been there since the fifties. I pulled up a stool at the counter, and the owner passed me a newspaper and slopped coffee into my cup without asking.

The old guy sat down right next to me a minute or so later, I had seen him and his hand-carved cane coming up the sidewalk when I was parking. GWG jeans, a white Stanfield V-neck t-shirt under a faded red and blue plaid jacket, work boots with stainless steel starting to show at the toes where the leather was worn through. Clean-shaven. Export 'A' cigarette pack peeking out of his breast pocket. I know this kind of man. He has worked hard every day of his life. Paid his bills. Buried his wife. He keeps his garage spotless, draws outlines of hammers in black felt pen on the pegboard above his workbench, repairs the lawnmower of the single lady next door, even though he doesn't like her noisy kids. My father will be this kind of man one day, sooner than I would like to admit.

The owner smiled hello at the old guy. "Soup of the day and pie with ice cream after?"

The old-timer nodded, and then spun his stool around to address the two older ladies tucked into the first booth by the door. "Bea. Helen. Enjoying the sunshine?"

They smiled, exchanged niceties, and then he turned back to me, squinting at the headlines in the open newspaper in front of me. "No good news in there, I read it this morning."

We get to talking. He asks me what I am doing in town, as it is painfully obvious to all of us that I am not from there. I tell him I am a writer, in town to teach some creative writing classes at the high school.

"Ah, an educated man then?" He narrows his eyes at me and then smiles, as if to let me know he will not hold this against me, even though he should.

I shrug. We move on and talk about other things. As far as I can tell, he continues to think I am a young man. I can tell by his comfortable body language, how he slaps me in the upper arm with the back of a gnarled hand when I crack a joke, the kinds of questions he asks me. The details about his own life he reveals.

Some people would say that I am being dishonest, that I am lying, to not stop him mid-sentence and inform him, even though he has not asked me, that according to what he has been taught to believe about these things, I am female. The people who believe that I am being deceitful have never lived in a skin like mine. I answer his questions with the truth. I mind my pronouns, sure, but I do not lie. Ever. Why? Because I like this old man, and so far, he likes me. Even if I am an educated man.

He tells me that his wife has been dead for ten years. That he is about to turn eighty-one years old. That he hates golf, and doesn't watch hockey. I ask him how many grandchildren he has. He has to think for a minute, moving his fingers in front of his face to count them. Ten he says. All of them turned out pretty okay, except for the one grandson, the druggie, who is sponging off his only daughter, can't keep a job.

I ask him what kind of drugs his grandson is on, and talk a little about my friend, the one I haven't seen in years, and her battles with the meth.

"Does she look hard now?" he asks me, and I think about this for a minute. "You know, older than her years? The drugs, they hit the ladies in the face harder than they do the fellas." He shakes his head, sadly. "Can make it hard to come back from." He holds up one finger, to make a point. "The hard stuff, I'm talking about here. Not the pot. I'll even take a bit of pot myself, now and then, for the arthritis, you know," he winks at me, "but I don't seem to get the same kick off the stuff I used to get. Maybe I'm toking it all wrong, who knows? Anyway, point is, I always stayed off the hard stuff, and now here I am, outliving everyone."

His pie and ice cream comes, and his coffee cup is refilled. We are both quiet for a minute while he eats.

"Don't get me wrong." He clears his throat, pushes his

plate away. "I'm no angel. I like my beer, for one thing. But if I was to give you any kind of decent advice, here is what I would say: stay off the hard stuff. By that I mean the hard liquor, the hard drugs, and especially the hard women." He laughs at his own joke then, slaps me on the back with a leathery paw.

I tell him it was great meeting him, and we shake hands. I am thankful for the weightlifting, and the calluses it gives me. As I push the glass door open to leave, he picks up his coffee cup and slides into the booth with his two lady friends. "Just having a little chat with a young fella from the city," he explains. "A writer, he tells me. Just telling him about my secret to sticking around long enough to get to be an old bastard like me."

I Will

We pick up the rings next week. We drop off the cheque for the florist tomorrow. My custom suit is hanging in my closet, and her dress is nearly finished. It is really happening. We are getting married.

I have learned a lot about what other people think about marriage over the last few months. Next to birth and death, I think it is one of the most ritualized things we do as humans, and people have strong feelings about it. They have ideas. I quickly learned that whenever one of my friends confessed that they were surprised I was getting married, it was because they thought my marriage would mirror what their idea of marriage looked like. Which it often does not. My sweetheart and I have worked really hard to build the kind of relationship that we could live happily in, and this rarely involved tracing the blueprints of others.

This does not mean I am not open to hearing advice about the topic. In fact, last week I called around the family, as I do, and asked them for any words of marital wisdom. My grandmother is ninety-two, and she had a miserable marriage, followed by a passionate love affair, so I was interested in what she had to say, having lived through the extremes. She told me to "foster the ability to really talk to each other. You don't want to know all of his secrets, but honour the ones that he does tell you. And respect each other. Respect is almost a bigger word for love."

Respect turned out to factor big in my family. My Uncle Rob told me to "make sure to marry your best friend. Respect her. You can love all kinds of stuff, you can love ice cream, you can love your new shoes, love is the most misused word in the world. When you respect something, you take care of it. Respect her, and take care of her. Be her best friend. And remember, everybody fucks up. Especially you. You come from a bloodline that is prone to selfishness and narcissism, so keep that in mind. Everybody screws up, but it is probably mostly going to be you."

My Aunt Cathy took the phone away from him to add: "Learn to nod your head when they talk about the boat or the motorhome or whatever. Be kind to each other, don't fight over stupid things. When Rob and I first got married he told me he would make all the big decisions and I would make all the little ones. So far we haven't had any big decisions."

Then she passed him back the phone. I asked Rob how long they had been married. "Near forty years if you count the time we were living in sin."

That would make them both experts, in my book.

My parents were married for twenty-six years, and my mom has been with her beau now for eight. She told me to "be honest with your feelings but always kind delivering the message. And you have to have fun. Laugh together a lot. And let him win once in a while."

Her partner Chuck chimed in from the living room, in the background: "Always make sure to have the last word. They should be 'Yes, dear.'"

They were both still laughing about this when they hung up the phone.

My cousin Dan and his wife Sarah have been married for thirteen years. I was interested in their opinions, being from the same generation, and similar radical lefty feministy artistic bent that we come from. Their words echoed those of the previous generations, almost exactly. Communication, always talking about problems before they really become an issue.

"Actively pursuing interests together," Dan says. "Show an interest in her interests. If I hadn't started learning about roller derby, who knows where we'd be by now? I get her to chase me on my bike on her skates. It's a good time for everyone. Even bystanders."

I called my Dad's wife Pat on the phone. She was my Dad's childhood sweetheart, and then her family moved away and they lost touch for thirty years. She stayed in love with him that whole time, and they reconnected on his fiftieth birthday, when she tracked him down and called him. They have been married now for fourteen years.

Pat had a one-word answer for me. "Trust," she said, without hesitation. I asked her how she stayed in love with my Dad for three decades, without even talking to him or seeing him. "I don't know. I can't answer that. I do know that the first time I saw him after all those years, it all just came rushing back into me. Where I kept it all that time, I cannot say."

My father's advice was very practical. He told me to "stay busy. She will get tired of vacuuming around you eventually."

When pressed, not a single member of my family thought that a queer marriage would need a different set of values than their straight ones. "A relationship is a relationship is a relationship," my grandmother informed me. "Whether you've got a piece of paper from the government or not. It is your marriage. You get to make the rules."

I found it interesting that none of my family even brought up things like co-habitation, or enforced monogamy, or rigid gender roles, or "settling down," which were all assumptions made by the predominately queer friends who expressed their shock over our upcoming wedding.

I do lament that I don't have three generations of queer married couples on hand to look to for marriage advice, as it hasn't been legal for long enough to afford us that. Maybe thirty years from now, we'll have a lot more to say to each other about queer marriage than "I never thought it would happen to you."

IVAN E. COYOTE is a writer, performer, and author of six previous books published by Arsenal Pulp Press, the most recent of which is *Missed Her*. Ivan is also the co-editor (with Zena Sharman) of the anthology *Persistence: All Ways Butch and Femme*. One of her stories appears in the anthology *It Gets Better*, edited by Dan Savage and Terry Miller.